S0-AEL-976

RAPTOR

Paul Zindel

MAYVILLE PUBLIC LIBRARY
MAYVILLE, NORTH DAKOTA
18,230

HYPERION BOOKS FOR CHILDREN
NEW YORK

ACKNOWLEDGMENTS

I wish to thank my brave friends Paula Danziger and Elizabeth Levy for teaching me what badlands, quicksand, and monsters to avoid. Much appreciation to my editor Erin McCormack Molta, who knows the secret lore of perilous watering holes and game trails—and without whom this book would not exist. Thanks to Lisa Holton, Lauren L. Wohl, and all my new extended family at Disney/Hyperion. Much thanks to Dorothy Neeley and my wonderful friends and students at Battle Mountain Junior High; also, appreciation to Ellen Rubin; Phyllis Minsch; Mary Beth Spore and Teri Lesesne; Julie Rusnak at Jakarta International School for arranging my visits to Balinese monkey forests and the secret lairs of Komodo dragons; Bandana Sen, Sara Zitto, and Patricia Sonnet at the American Embassy School who let me ride elephants and motorcycles in India; Gracelyn Fina Shea; Kathleen Miksis; Lucretia Lipper; the extraordinary brain engineers (librarians) Cindy Dobrez and Lynn Rutan; Hiroshi Kander; much appreciation for the dinosaur research and native American Scholarship of Professor Richard Cahill; thanks to author Dona Schenker; and my friends Kevin Rose, Sam Havens, Sue Spaniol.

And special thanks to: my son, David; my daughter, Lizabeth; Mr. Ellis's terrific kids at I.S. 34; and Gothal, the good and beloved witch.

Copyright © 1998 by Paul Zindel.
Jacket illustration © 1998 by Daniel Horne.

All rights reserved. No part of this book may be reproduced or transmitted in any form or by any means, electronic or mechanical, including photocopying, recording, or by any information storage and retrieval system, without written permission from the publisher. For information address Hyperion Books for Children, 114 Fifth Avenue, New York, New York 10011-5690.

First Edition
1 3 5 7 9 10 8 6 4 2

The text for this book is set in 14-point Bembo.
Library of Congress Cataloging-in-Publication Data:

Zindel, Paul.
Raptor / Paul Zindel. — 1st ed.
p. cm.
Summary: Zack and his Ute Indian friend find themselves trapped in a cave with a living dinosaur— the deadly Utahraptor.
ISBN 0-7868-0338-X (trade)—ISBN 0-7868-2374-7 (lib. ed.)
1. Utahraptor—Juvenile fiction. [1. Utahraptor—Fiction.
2. Dinosaurs—Fiction. 3. Survival—Fiction.] I. Title.
PZ10.3.Z263Rap 1998
[Fic]—dc21 98-5330

CONTENTS

To Spencer Manley Ellis

RAPTOR

THE NEST

Flaming Gorge, Utah

*P*rofessor Norak stopped dead in his tracks. This must be a joke, he thought. A few of his paleontology students were playing a joke. Very funny.

He'd told everyone at the main dig that he was going to spend his day off exploring the caves and abandoned silver mine north of the dam. Two of the summer interns had already shown their twisted senses of humor by greasing up a bunch of triceratops gizzard stones and slipping them into a girl's sleeping bag. The girl was one of those neatness freaks and she had run through the whole camp screaming. The professor could easily imagine the same kids stealing into the mine the night before and using chisels to fake the scratching, raking,

1

and kicking marks. He had to laugh. They had made the imprints from talon feet much too large.

"Quite a joke," he told Mario, his pack mule, as he examined the "dinosaur nest." The animal turned from the edge of darkness to stare at Professor Norak. It pawed at the ground, shuddered from a tick bite, then tried to tug its reins loose from the base of a stalagmite.

Somewhere below—in the bowels of the network of rotting mine shafts and solution caves that riddled Silver Mountain—the murky shape of a mother lizard was looking for food near the base of a waterfall. She had searched for hours each day, ever since she'd felt motion beginning inside her eggs in the nest—a warning that there would soon be a dozen hatchlings clawing at her underside for food. Her instincts had told her it was time to gorge on blind mud fish and stubby-limbed bats—anything she could find hiding in the dark and damp crannies of the caves.

Today she grazed along the edge of a subterranean stream, letting her heat-sensing tongue slip from the end of her snout. Suddenly, her tongue felt a hot, burning sensation near a cluster of rocks. She swung her weight onto one foot and kicked the pile violently aside. A visiting family of plump otters snarled and screamed and scrambled toward the cave stream—but the mother lizard was too fast for them. Her snout shot quickly left, then right, her jaws catching the otters by their heads, crushing each skull as though it were a grape. The burst of dripping warm brains soothed the back of her throat but baited her day's hunger.

When the last of the otters lay still and mutilated on the rocks, the mother lizard allowed herself to eat the fattest carcass. When she had finished, she leisurely chewed and swallowed the bloody pulp and bones of the others into her storage stomach. Soon she would regurgitate the half-digested feasts—to vomit strength and energy into the eager mouths of her brood.

Professor Norak knelt for a closer look at the "nest." A sharp, fetid smell tore up into his nostrils. Oh, you're good, he thought about the student culprits. You must have laughed yourselves silly imitating a mother raptor building her nest. The marks from her birth ritual. A scattering of vegetation at the fringes as she would have set her hind legs, rigidly holding on to the rim with deadly front claws.

The light from a single Coleman lamp cast the shadows of Professor Norak and the mule high onto a quartz-veined wall. Mario snorted, drooled, and began to sidestep like a crab.

"A mother dinosaur would have laid her eggs, spread a last layer of greenery, then straddled the mound." Professor Norak spoke softly to the mule, trying to calm it. "She'd have snuggled and gently lowered her swollen belly. Her body heat would have generated steam. Ammonia. Decaying fern. Vapors drifting in the mine wind."

SCRATCH. SCRAAAATCH.

Norak heard the distant sounds of scraping on stone and gravel being moved. A raccoon or possum, he thought. His hand touched something oval in the nest.

He laughed out loud.

Eggs!

He could see his students shopping in a toy store, checking all the footballs and toss-toys they could marinate to look like the perfect dozen "dinosaur eggs."

SCRAAAATCH . . .

More sounds. Something was approaching from one of the rear passages of the mine.

Something bigger than a raccoon.

A coyote, the professor thought now. A coyote or a bear that called the abandoned mine and caves its home. *Or the sounds could be scratchings from hiding, giggling interns.*

4

"Hello," Professor Norak called out to the blackness. "I'm on to your little hoax!"

No one answered.

A new, nauseating smell hit him. The mule began to bray and try to shake the bit from its mouth. "Take it easy, good buddy," Norak said, standing as he held tightly to the single glistening egg. He went to pat the animal and assure it—but it spooked. Its hooves shot high into the air tumbling a cluster of stones and crashing the Coleman lamp to the floor. The light began to flicker.

"Whoa," the professor said. He fumbled to fix the lamp.

THUMP.

Another sound from the labyrinth of tunnels and caves was louder and closer. There came more scratching. A slight chill grabbed Norak in spite of himself. He tried to laugh it off, but now there were vibrations beneath his feet, as though a truck were barreling toward him.

CLOSER.

Big deal. A cassette player, the professor told himself. The interns had probably set speakers all over the place. Woofers and tweeters from any electronics store. It had to be all part of the prank. Still, Norak clutched the egg and started to retreat. He would return to the main dig and then send an Indian worker back for the mule. He began to jog toward the mine's exit. It was a prank. A very elaborate prank.

There was the flapping of small wings, and shrewlike mammals darted near his feet. Tiny green lizards appeared on the walls—spindly-legged chameleons with long tails and dark-crested eyebrows. The contacts of the lamp held for a moment. Norak looked behind him. He glimpsed the mule bucking madly.

Tethered.

Suddenly, beyond the animal, an enormous form began to emerge from the darkness. He saw a bounding shadow of pebbled, leathery skin racing toward him. It was the shape of a creature familiar to him from text-books and years of exhuming bones. A thing he had studied his whole life.

Oh, God. Oh, God . . .

A scream erupted from deep inside Norak as the creature began to run upright with shining eyes, a flash of teeth, and its stiff tail protruding behind it.

A raptor!

Something extinct!

Norak believed he was hallucinating. It was heatstroke or a rapture from the mine gas. His chest heaved with painful gasps as the raptor propelled itself forward with thick, powerful hind legs. Its enormous body cut a swath through twisted fingers of limestone. Its mouth was open revealing jaws the size of a bull crocodile and the serrated fangs of a meat eater.

Shrieking, the raptor pounced on Mario, seizing the mule by its throat. The animal bleated as the raptor balanced on one hind leg, then quickly lifted its other leg high into the air. It thrust a single large claw into the mule's underbelly, exploding blood and entrails out onto the ground.

Again the claw was lifted and swung.

And again.

Within seconds, the carcass was reduced to a steaming, shredded heap of lymph and muscles and bowels. The raptor clamped its jaws onto one of Mario's legs and shook the carcass like a rag doll. Blood splashed over the cave wall until the leg was ripped free. The raptor's neck expanded as it swallowed it whole.

Norak ran as in a nightmare. The Coleman lamp was dead now, and he hurled it away. There was light at the end of the mine shaft. His mind was out of control. A *Utahraptor!*

Alive!

Real!

He thought the creature would stop, believed it would stay at its nest and protect its eggs.

ROAR.

It was after him, with shreds of Mario's intestines hanging from its mouth.

The ground behind Norak shook. He tripped and fell near the end of the tunnel. There was a snorting above, and he was lifted into the air, his legs dangling. The raptor held him with its small but muscular forelimbs, and began to turn him like a spider examining a fly. Norak felt the creature's hot, stinking breath. He looked up hopelessly into the face.

The raptor cocked its head to stare at him with outsized glassy eyes.

ROAR.

A thick green froth dripped from the bony slabs that were its lips. The raptor pinned him with a forearm against a slab of quartz. It slammed its free limb into the crystal, shattering it into a web of ruptures. Slowly, it slid a claw gently down the left side of Norak's face.

Norak's body shook. Sweat poured from the pits of his arms as he looked into the cold, dark eyes of the monster.

Jesus, help me. . . . Baby Jesus, help me. . . .

He realized he was still clutching the egg!

With a single, violent headshake, the raptor's teeth ripped the shirt from his body. Norak felt terrible pain now, as the raptor slowly pushed the point of its claw up into his chin. The tip moved higher, piercing a neck gland, then up into his gums like a thick dentist's needle. Norak's mouth filled with blood, and the world tilted madly.

ANOTHER ROAR.

Louder.

Deafening.

The ground and the walls around them began to shake and crumble. Chunks of dirt and stone and rotting beams fell away from the mouth of the tunnel. Suddenly, Norak was aware of sunlight crashing into the blackness. The earth opened up. The raptor dropped him, and he was falling.

Rolling.

Only now, the egg slipped from his grasp. He covered his face as branches of sagebrush ripped into his arms. In his last conscious moment, he heard the escalating scream of an avalanche and glimpsed the bloodied, disembodied head of his mule tumbling past him.

KILLING GROUNDS

*T*hat was your mom," Mrs. Rosario called to Zack as she hung up the phone. "She wants you to meet her at the Dry Lakes airstrip. Pronto! Your father's been in an accident."

Zack shoved the cooking spatula into the head grill chef's hand. "What happened?" he yelled as he tore off his cooking apron and grabbed for his safety helmet.

"A rockslide," Mrs. Rosario said. "He's been hurt badly."

Zack was out the screen door of the Chile Cafe and into the parking lot. *Don't let him be in pain*, he prayed for his father as he locked the helmet strap under his chin. He jumped onto his Yamaha 120, hit the kick starter, and the motor shrieked to life. He rode high until speed and the wind had cooled the leather seat down from the scorching badlands' sun. Moving to Utah was a mistake, Zack had told his family from the beginning. A really *big* mistake.

"Move it," Zack yelled at a herd of cattle taking its time crossing a gulch. He braked, and punched the horn. Its loud honk was met by angry belching from the animals as they climbed a grass-clumped dune. He opened the throttle, jerked the front wheel of the motorcycle into the air for a moment, and then sped onward. The bike kicked up a dust cloud that trailed from the Jensen service road as far as the Drive Through the Ages—the paved tourist highway north.

This whole dig in Utah was an accident waiting to happen, Zack thought. In fact, it was an accident of nature—millions of years before—that had made the northeast corner of the state famous. A mountain had exploded and created a vast cloud of volcanic ash, a death cloud that had snuffed out the lives of thousands—millions!—of dinosaurs. Roaming among the landscape of monstrous skeletons were mobs of photo-starved tourists and save-the-whale students and geeky, stuck-up paleontologists who journeyed from all over the world to see a bunch of bones left behind by what turned out to be the complete extermination of the "terrible lizards" of Utah.

RRRMMMM!

Zack revved the motorcycle up to forty. Driving each day from his home to work at the Chile Cafe had taught him every inch of the south network of arroyos and washes. There were stretches that reminded Zack of what Mars must look like, miles upon miles strewn with yellow-gray mounds of stone and tilted, isolated buttes that rose sharply out of the valleys and naked hills. He'd taken brief drives to the north and glimpsed its vast, unexplored canyons and forests. There were gorges with eerie names like Disaster Falls and Screaming Wolf.

He had read his father's textbooks and seen drawings of creatures wiped out at the edge of a prehistoric swamp. Dinosaur National Monument was a Pompeii of predators like *T. rex*, the flesh-eating Tyrant Lizard King, and thousands of *Deinonychus*—also known as raptors. Entombed beside them, in the main quarry, were the bones of large herbivores, plant eaters like *Diplodocus* and *Apatosaurus*.

Bad thoughts.

Lately, Zack had been having nothing but bad thoughts about the university dig and his family's move from Los Angeles. "Give it a chance," his father had insisted. "If I'd been offered a job in L.A., I would have taken it."

Most everyone working on the project was egomaniacal, especially Dr. Boneid, the head paleontologist on the dig. Boneid loved, if had not invented, his nickname: Dr. Bones.

"He's a death spirit," Zack had heard one of the old Ute Indian workers say about him. "His heart is like death."

Zack flashed on a memory of Boneid. "HOW DARE YOU! HOW *DARE* YOU!" the raving paleontologist had screamed. Zack's father had made the mistake of mentioning to a reporter visiting the quarry that he'd found a new fossil of an extremely rare late Cretaceous palm.

"No one talks to the press—except ME! You try that again and you're out of here, you amateur!" Boneid had shrieked. Zack had felt the anguish of his father's humiliation as he watched him leave Boneid's tent and walk past a half dozen silent workers and colleagues. Boneid had come out after his father. He wasn't finished with him. Zack had stopped him in his tracks.

"Don't yell at my father," Zack had said. "You don't have the right to yell at anyone."

"Mind your own business."

"You're lucky to have him on this dig."

"He's lucky to have a job."

"Treat him professionally," Zack had warned, "or I'll report you to the union."

Boneid had glared at him. "Oh, so you're a trouble-maker just like your father. A chip off the old block."

"You bet I am," Zack had said. He had watched Boneid's thin blue lips curl into a smile as he turned and went back into his trailer.

Zack had been working on the dig helping to set up the bullet hammer, a heavy steel device designed to fire shotgun shells into the quarry bordering the national dinosaur park. The sound waves resonated straight down through hundreds of feet of the rock and sand layers, then reflected back up to register seismic pictures of ancient buried beasts. His job was exciting, but watching the daily shame of his father was more than he could take. The last thing he said to Boneid when he quit to fry hamburgers at the Chile Cafe was, *"Treat him with respect. You treat my father with respect or you'll regret it."*

Zack spotted his mother standing in the shade of a shed at the edge of the airstrip. She looked ghostly in white makeup broken only by a slash of black lipstick. Next to her, his father lay secured to a stretcher on the bed of a 4x4 truck. Several workers from the Uintah Reservation watched and waited beneath the branches of a lone pine.

Mrs. Norak watched Zack speed toward them as a noisy twin-engine Cessna touched down on the airstrip.

The medical plane, its engines roaring, blasted clouds of sand and dust as it taxied from the far end of the field. Zack raced the plane to his mother.

"Glad you made it," his mom said.

Zack jumped off the bike and leaned it against the truck. "Is Dad going to be okay?"

"I think so. There was a rockslide," Mrs. Norak said. "He fell down one of the gorges. A couple of the Indians found him. They brought him into Vernal. His left leg was broken. Dr. Morrison set it, but there are head injuries. He needs a CAT scan. The closest machines are at Mormon Hospital in Salt Lake City."

Zack took off his helmet and swung up onto the bed of the truck. His father's eyes were closed and his chest was rising and falling from rapid, desperate breaths.

"I'll go with you," Zack said.

"No," Mrs. Norak said. "There won't be room for you on the plane. Besides, it's better if you stay at the house. Take care of the dog and anything that comes up. I'll send for you if I need you."

Zack noticed a bloody mark beneath his father's chin. "What's that?"

"Dr. Morrison said it looked as though he'd fallen on a spike or wooden stake in the mine." Anger crept into his mother's voice. "I told him to stay out of the north caves. That old mine up there has shafts that drop fifteen hundred feet. He's lucky he's not dead." The door of the plane opened, and she walked out to meet the pilot and paramedic.

Professor Norak's eyes slowly opened. Zack held his hand.

"Hi, Dad," Zack said.

Norak looked at his son, his eyes searching about as if to see if anyone else was listening. His lips moved, and Zack leaned closer.

"What, Dad?"

"The girl," Professor Norak said, straining to be heard. "I . . . told the girl." A shaking finger.

Zack looked to an old rusted Jeep parked a hundred yards away near a cluster of juniper trees. He recognized Uta, a young Indian girl with dark bronze skin and straight black hair that fell to her waist. She'd been in a few of his classes at the local high school when he had transferred near the end of the term. They'd been assigned to do a science fair experiment together and sort of hung out sometimes. So far, she was the only thing good about Utah.

Uta's uncle, Larry Ghost Coyote, his face shriveled from a lifetime of badlands sun, circled the Jeep kicking dried clumps of mud off its tires.

"I told *her* . . . ," Zack's father said, his voice breaking.

"Told her what?"

Norak's voice faded in and out. "I found it . . . something impossible. It dropped. You must find it, Zack. . . . Please find it. . . ." He began to moan and his eyes rolled high up into his head showing only the whites. Tremors shook his body.

"Help him!" Zack yelled to the medic. "He's having a convulsion! Help!"

Mrs. Norak and the paramedic came running with a cart of supplies. The medic thrust his fingers into the professor's mouth to keep his throat open and stop him from swallowing his own tongue. He pressed the end of a stethoscope against the professor's heaving chest.

"It's shock," the paramedic said, thrusting an intravenous line in his arm. "He'll be okay. Get him to the plane."

Mrs. Norak snapped her fingers at two of the Indian workers. They lifted the stretcher and carried Professor Norak toward the Cessna. Zack walked fast at his father's side. The dark brown centers of his eyes fluttered back down into place.

"I'm here," Zack said.

His father strained to look at him. A speck of gray had caked at the edge of his lips.

"Find it . . ." his father whispered.

"Find *what?*" Zack asked.

"You'll know . . ."

A mask of terror crawled onto Professor Norak's face as his hand reached up to the wound on his chin. He remembered something more. "DON'T GO IN THE CAVE! DON'T GO IN!"

Now he was screaming.

Uta watched Zack waving good-bye as the Cessna took off toward the Shining Mountains. He was tense with worry, shielding his eyes from the low afternoon sun. She herself had made the trip a few times on the medical plane when there had been chain-saw accidents and other emergencies at the reservation. She knew the plane would fly over the Uintas wilderness. There would be Heber City, then Alta, and a sharp banking north of the distant Skull Valley Reservation before the plane drifted into the landing corridor for Salt Lake City.

Zack gave a last wave good-bye and walked his motorcycle toward her. "Uta!" he called. "You found my father?"

The girl, using her fingers to comb her hair to one side of her face, walked to meet him. Uta had liked him the second she'd seen his narrow, handsome face last spring. His wolflike eyes had reminded her of photos she'd seen of her own father when he was young and wore braids and danced her tribe's dances in bearskins and buffalo hides. Somehow she knew that she wanted to be his friend. She didn't care if he grew a long beard or three heads. Just the sight of him had caused a quickening of her blood.

"You know my uncle, Larry Ghost Coyote," she said. "We were scouting wild ponies above the power dam. On the way back, we saw the fresh rockslide on Silver Mountain. Your dad had broken bones."

Zack's words caught in his throat. "You . . . you saved his life," he said. He gave Uta a hug, and shook Larry Ghost Coyote's hand long and hard. "Thanks for finding him. He wouldn't have lasted alone out there." Zack had worked with Larry Ghost Coyote the few weeks he'd spent on the dig.

Larry saw Zack's eyes were glistening. He had seen him working at his father's side. He'd watched them sharing lunches together, laughing, and knew how close they were.

"Bad scratches," Larry Ghost Coyote said. "We got him out of the heat."

"The shocks are on the Jeep are shot," Uta apologized. "Your dad was burning up. It was like he had sunstroke. We got him to drink some water, but he kept mumbling about something he'd left behind. He couldn't tell us what it was." Uta swung her hair now so it all hung straight down her back. "But he wanted you to find it."

Zack took a deep breath and glanced back to the sky. He saw the speck of the medical plane disappearing over the ridge of mountains to the west. He remembered his father's face.

Desperate.

Frightened.

He asked Uta, "Could you take me back to where you found him?"

"When?"

"Could we go now on my bike?"

Uta looked up to check the sun. She spoke quickly to her uncle in Ute. The sound of the language was soft, like a mixture of Spanish and Aztec. When she turned back to Zack, she said, "I told my uncle we're going. You can drop me off at the reservation later, okay?"

"Sure," Zack said. He swung an arm around Larry Ghost Coyote's shoulder. "Thanks again for saving my pop," he said.

Larry smiled at him and climbed up behind the wheel of his Jeep. He started the motor, gave them both a wave, and drove straight down the center of the airstrip toward the Uinta River.

Zack grabbed the spare helmet out of a rear saddlebag and tossed it to Uta. She put it on and straddled the passenger seat with her arms around Zack's waist. She felt his stomach muscles tighten as he kicked the starter. "Hold on," Zack said, opening the throttle. The wheels spun in the dirt, then grabbed, and the bike shot forward.

They drove north along the arroyos and streams edging the Drive Through the Ages. Within a few miles, the sagebrush and dwarf piñon trees gave way to stands of ponderosa pine and moss-covered rock. Jackrabbits and a lone mule deer bolted across the roadway.

Uta inched forward on her seat. "How come your motor is so quiet? My brothers let me drive their old Harleys and they sound like crop-dusting planes."

"I had a special muffler and converter extension welded on. Its cruising noise is pretty low."

Uta laughed. "You're always tinkering with something, aren't you!" She pointed the way from the southern tip of the Flaming Gorge Reservoir until the roadway crossed over the power dam. The downstream rim of the dam was a low stone wall with a huge drop-off into a roaring spillway. Zack kept the bike near the center line of the road. "You'd better hold on tight. It would really suck to have an accident up here."

Uta looked at the drop-off and shuddered. Suddenly, Zack deliberately swerved the bike and she screamed. Zack laughed.

21

"You're sick," Uta said, managing to laugh with him. "Really sick."

"Yeah," Zack said proudly. "I know. Imagine falling seven hundred feet!"

"Actually, it's only five hundred and ten feet. I used to work summers as a dam tour guide," Uta said. "I had lots of nightmares that I'd trip, fall in, and be chopped up in the turbine blades."

Uta pointed Zack away from the reservoir and farther north. The trees cast long shadows now and the setting sun transformed the mountains ahead into dark, looming giants. "Are we close?" Zack asked.

"There!" Uta cried out.

Zack looked ahead to where a wash cut into a narrow canyon. The bike's motor strained to climb the sharp incline. Halfway up he saw an entrance to the abandoned silver mine. The debris of the rockslide spilled down a hundred feet from its mouth. Zack followed the ruts left by the SUVs of mineral hunters. He parked the bike, and he and Uta hiked up to the edge of the spill.

"How do we know we won't set off another avalanche?" Zack asked.

Uta looked up to the high ground. "I think we'll be okay. I've climbed around these hills half my life. This spot seems to have spent its energy. She pointed. "Your dad was up there. Lucky the avalanche wasn't any bigger or no one would have found him."

Zack climbed to the area and kicked aside a few of the rocks. Uta hiked up the left side of the spill to where a cloud of flies hovered.

Buzzzzz.

"Shoo! Shoo, bugs!" she said, swatting at them. Something was glistening from under a cluster of stones, and she knelt down to take a closer look.

She screamed.

Zack scrambled to her side. "What?"

She pointed.

He looked down at the ground. A pair of swollen, clouded eyes were staring up at him. The sickening odor of rotting flesh socked up into his nostrils. His eyes watered as he kicked away stones until he'd exposed the head of the mule.

"Jeez," Uta said. "Your father wanted you to find *this*?"

"I don't think so."

Uta took a stick and probed around the severed neck bone.

"And you think *I'm* sick?" Zack said.

"Hey, it looks like it was cut off like with a guillotine."

"The skin's shredded." Zack knelt to look closer. He saw splinters of skull and a series of slashing cuts across the animal's ears. The neck wound was oozing a foaming, slimy fluid.

"What is that gook?" Uta asked.

"It looks like spit."

"Saliva?"

"It looks like something bit it."

"Bit its head off?"

"I didn't say that," Zack said.

The stench was terrible now. They backed away and the swarm of flies scooted back to feast and lay their eggs. Zack looked farther up the slope. He saw something white lying near the mine entrance. He climbed up to what looked like a half-deflated balloon.

"What is it?"

Zack knelt beside the oval shape. "I'm not sure. It looks like some kind of an egg."

"An *egg*?"

Zack poked it. "A very *big* egg."

"Can't be. Eggs don't get that big."

"It could be from an ostrich."

"This is Utah, not Australia."

"Doesn't matter. Lots of people have started ostrich farms all over the United States now. It's supposed to be like steak without the fat. Healthy and a good investment—and worth a lot of money." He slipped his hands gently under the egg and lifted it. "I'm taking it."

Uta cleared her throat. "I don't think you should."

"Why not?"

"It's something my family taught me," Uta said. "My tribe. Whatever it is, it belongs here and we shouldn't mess with it."

"This is what my father was talking about," Zack said. "Don't you see? He wanted me to get it!" Zack stood up cradling the egg, and started back down the slope toward the bike.

"Well, if you think I'm holding it on the ride home, you're crazy."

Zack slid the egg under his T-shirt and tucked the bottom of the shirt tight into his jeans. He reached the bike and climbed on, leaving the plump, long oval resting in the makeshift stomach sling.

"A potbelly is very becoming on you," Uta said, climbing onto the bike behind him.

"Hold on." Zack started the motor and revved the throttle. The bike lurched forward.

Uta grabbed his shoulders as they started down the rutted slope. Before they reached the paved road, Zack glanced back for a last look. A half moon had begun to rise over the mountain, and he could swear he heard the faint screams of his father echo off the jagged rock face.

SOUNDS

*T*he headlight of the motorcycle was a cyclops's eye shooting a beam of light several hundred feet through the darkness ahead of them. Zack shifted uncomfortably in his seat. "I think it's leaking," he said as they reached the south end of the Drive Through the Ages. "The egg. It's leaking something . . . gooey."

Uta tried to hold back her laughter.

"I'd better drop it off at my house," Zack said. "Then I'll drive you home. Okay?"

"I'm in no rush." She held on tight as they made a sharp turn and raced up a desolate dirt road. Zack felt his stomach rolling. "There's meatballs and lasagna and stuff if you're interested in something to eat."

"Sounds like a plan."

The road edged by a pond at the base of rolling hills. When they reached the Noraks' ranch house, Zack's dog, Picasso, was already barking his head off inside. Zack parked under a breezeway, clutched at the bulge in his wet T-shirt, and ran inside. Picasso scampered about at his feet, wagging his tail and jumping up on his legs.

"Easy, boy, easy," Zack said. He flicked on lights and headed for the hall bathroom. When Picasso saw Uta, he growled.

"Lay off, Picasso!" Zack yelled.

"Don't you remember me, Picasso?" Uta asked the scraggly white poodle. Picasso barked louder. "What a tough guy!" she said. "You don't scare me. I know all your tricks."

Uta stopped at the edge of the sprawling living room. It had a massive granite fireplace, a worn leather sofa, and a couple of rattan chairs with big paisley pillows. She'd been to the house several times when she and Zack had collaborated on the science project. They had called their exhibit *The Effect of Direct Current on Seedlings.* Zack had joked that it should have been titled *An Electric Chair for Lima Beans.* They'd worked long hours at the kitchen table, soldering electrode grids into petri dishes and plotting growth charts. They'd had fun working together and got an A, to boot.

Picasso stopped barking and began to sniff at her ankles and wag his stubby tail. "Now you remember me, don't you?" Uta said, petting him.

In the bathroom, Zack took the sticky egg and laid it in the white porcelain tub. He took off his shirt, tossed it into the hamper, and began wiping the slime off his stomach with a washcloth. "Hey, Uta, can you feed Picasso, please?" he shouted into the house intercom. "The dog food's under the sink. He gets half a can."

"Okay." Uta's voice came from the speaker.

"The meatballs for us are in the fridge."

Zack heard Uta rattling pots and pans as he checked himself in the mirror. His lips and mouth were dry, and he was about to brush his teeth when he heard a squishing sound. Out of the corner of his eye he saw the egg moving. He dropped down on his knees to get a closer look.

"Hey, it's moving," Zack yelled out. "The egg is *moving!*"

"Great," Uta's voice came out of the intercom. "Let me know when you're the proud father of an ostrich."

Zack stared at the egg. Fluid from it was shooting out in quick, short spurts. He reached out and prodded it with the tip of a comb. A single green claw shot up through the hole and began tugging at the comb.

"Hey, Uta, you'd better get in here," Zack called. "Don't think it's an ostrich."

Zack poked the egg again.

Squish.

A *second* claw broke out of the shell. The egg shuddered and rolled like a Mexican jumping bean as the tears widened. The rest of its slimy fluid burst out like shots from a water pistol.

"YEOOOW!" Zack yelled.

The claws tore away the covering and a wet pathetic little shape began to uncurl. It swelled and doubled in size as it shook and stretched free of its casing. Picasso came running into the room and jumped up, planting his paws on the rim of the tub. He saw the glistening, twitching hatchling and barked wildly.

Uta called from the kitchen. "Want your meatballs on a hero or with spaghetti?"

Zack didn't hear her. The hatchling unfurled until it was the size of a gnarled green chicken with a long tail. Picasso cocked his head and looked puzzled, then spun around and raced out of the bathroom.

The lizard lifted its quivering snout. It stared at Zack with enormous yellow eyes and opened its mouth to reveal teeth that protruded from its jaws like the tips of steak knives. A glob of slime shot from its throat and hit the shower wall.

"Nasty," Zack said. He grabbed a towel, and the creature stared intensely at him as he gently patted its skin. Another burst of projectile mucus flew into the air just missing Zack's face.

"Really nasty," Zack mumbled.

Uta stood in the doorway. "I've never seen a lizard like that before. It looks really weird." The creature looked at Uta and began hissing. Zack stroked the lizard's neck. "This has got to be what my dad was excited about. Maybe he knew he'd discovered a whole new species."

"What're you going to do with it?"

The hatchling opened its mouth as if yawning. Its long thin tongue slid out and licked Zack's hand. "Keep it until my dad gets back."

"Well, I'm starving." She turned, and went back to the kitchen. "I still think you should have left it alone," she called out as she rummaged for forks in a drawer. "It probably has a mother somewhere who's probably missing it."

Zack leaned over into the tub and scratched the hatchling's chest. Picasso sat in the doorway growling. "You rest awhile," Zack told the lizard. He started to leave when the hatchling made loud, desperate sounds.

HOOOONK. HONK. HONK.

The lizard jumped out of the tub and ran to Zack, rubbing its snout on his legs.

HONK. HONK.

"Hey, I think this thing likes me!" Zack called to Uta.

"Don't touch it. It could be poisonous!" Uta called. "Besides, it's probably imprinting on you, thinks you're its mother."

Zack came down the hall with the lizard scooting along at his heels. Picasso trailed trying to nip at it. The lizard stopped short and swung its crinkled head around to stare at the dog. It opened its mouth, bared its teeth, and let loose an earsplitting HONK. Picasso ran for his favorite toy, a rubber hot dog that squealed. He began shaking it crazily. The lizard spit at Picasso and screeched louder.

HONK. HONK.

"Spitting is impolite," Zack told the hatchling. He faked right, and the lizard headed right. He made a quick step left. It turned left.

Uta carried a plate of steaming spaghetti to the kitchen table. She set it down next to the meatballs, a basket of whole wheat bread, and a tub of butter. She saw Zack coming down the hall. "Did you figure out what *kind* of lizard it is?"

Zack looked closer at the hatchling. The back edge of its teeth were perfect for sawing meat. It began to sniff at the air like a hound, and moved more confidently now— walking totally upright on its thick, muscular haunches. It held its tail stiffly out behind like a balance, and its hips tilted backward like a bird's. A single large claw on each foot stood erect.

Uta saw the expression change on Zack's face.

"What's the matter?" she asked.

"I think it's a baby . . ."

Zack hesitated to say the word, knowing it was absurd. The lizard was in motion now, running toward the steaming platters. As it leaped up onto a kitchen chair, Zack knew it was the impossible.

"IT'S A RAPTOR!" Zack shouted. "A DINOSAUR!"

Uta screamed as the lizard plowed toward her with its mouth wide. It skidded to a halt at the center of the table, and began snapping at the plates. Meatballs scattered and bounced up into the air. The raptor's jaws gnashed, devouring everything they touched.

Uta grabbed her own plate of food and moved fast back against the wall. The creature thumped its tail down, used it like another leg as it sunk the large claw from its left foot into the spaghetti. The pasta and red sauce clung to the talons and splashed across the table.

"It can't be!" Uta cried out. "Dinosaurs are extinct!"

"*This* one isn't!"

The hatchling began tearing the tablecloth and eating the wicker of the bread basket.

"Stop it," Uta scolded as she threw her crumpled napkin at it.

Zack salvaged a few meatballs and pieces of bread that had slid onto a chair. He added them to Uta's plate and shoved it into the refrigerator. Within minutes, the raptor had picked the table clean, jumped down on the floor, and began snapping up the scraps and globs of hurled sauce.

Picasso spun in circles, barking.

"It's still hungry," Zack said.

"Sure," Uta said. "It hasn't eaten in a hundred and forty million years!"

"Here!" he shouted to the creature. Zack dashed into the pantry and opened the lid on a storage freezer. The raptor ran after him, jumped up, and began sinking its claws into frost-covered packages. Zack and Uta stood back and watched in shock as the raptor looked grateful and ripped off mouthful after mouthful of icy meat and fish sticks.

"It *can't* be . . . ," Uta said.

"Hey, I've seen sketches of what baby raptors were supposed to have looked like." He moved back into the kitchen, opened the refrigerator, and took out the plate of food he'd salvaged. Both he and Uta grabbed at the meatballs with their fingers. "You know what this means?" Zack whispered.

"No."

"It means my father's going to be rich and famous," Zack said, trembling with excitement. His mind was still trying to accept what his eyes saw. "He found a dinosaur. My dad found a dinosaur."

"He found the egg, but you hatched it."

"It's still his find. But maybe we'll all be famous!" Zack said. "And loaded! Our pictures will be in every paper in the world! We'll be on CNN and do fast-food commercials!"

HONK.

"Well, I still think you should have left the little honker where he belonged," Uta said.

Zack's eyes shone as he reached out to pet the raptor. "You know, that's a good name for him."

"What?"

The hatchling looked up as though he knew they were talking about him.

"*Honker.*"

The mother raptor searched frantically through the

mountain's caves. She had been confused by the intruder and the rockslide. Several of her huge saw-edged teeth had been chipped and she'd bruised one of her forearms. Already she could feel her body healing itself. Secondary teeth began to replaced damaged ones, growing swiftly like stalks from fertile garden bulbs.

Her first instinct was to safeguard the tunnels leading to her nest. She roared and lurched, sniffing through every side chamber and alcove. Then she traced and re-traced her steps, returning each time to count her eggs. Eleven. Each time when she returned she saw only eleven. Finally, she had calmed enough to know what had happened. She began to shriek, cries steeped in pain and sorrow and rage. Her body shook with anguish, and she withheld her body heat from her nest.

Night had fallen in the landscape beyond. She breathed deeply and dared to leave the mountain. She paused on the slope, letting the wind bring her all she'd need to know. Her nostrils, a hundred times more sensitive than a bloodhound's, detected the trail. She gave a last matri-archal roar before bounding down the slope, her jaws wide with fury.

Zack and Uta babbled nonstop as they cleaned up the kitchen and finally collapsed on the living room sofa.

Zack ignited the propane feed to the fireplace. After a while Picasso and Honker got tired of bickering, sprawled on the hearth, and began to nuzzle each other.

Uta asked, "Why are they rubbing their heads together?"

"Maybe it's the way dinos show affection."

"It's cute."

Zack went out to the kitchen and brought back the bone from a frozen leg of lamb. Honker and Picasso gnawed on it together.

The hall phone rang. Zack went to answer it. He was glad to hear his mother's voice. "Your dad's going to be okay," Mrs. Norak said, sounding very tired. Zack sighed with relief.

"He had some internal bleeding, so they had to operate—but he did fine. He's in the recovery room now. The stitches can come out in a week, but he's going to be on crutches for a while."

"Can I talk to him?"

"Not right now," his mother said. "They had to sedate him. He was screaming. It was so strange. He was wide awake but it was as though he was trapped in a nightmare. He'll have his own room in a few hours with a phone and TV and newspapers and all those things. He'll probably sleep the rest of the night, so we'll call you in the morning, okay, dear?"

Zack glanced over to Honker. He thought about telling his mother about the big secret, but he knew she'd think he was out of his mind. She'd freak out with worry and end up calling Dr. Bones or one of his assistants. The news of his father's discovery would get out, and his dad would end up with nothing. His dad had found the egg on his day off and far away from the official dig. It was his find, but that wouldn't matter. Bones'd take the credit for it, like he did everything else.

"Did Dad say anything about what happened?" Zack asked.

"No. His head injuries were pretty bad. The only thing the doctors were puzzled about was the scar under his chin. I told them he hadn't had it before he went into the cave. I know this sounds crazy, but they said it looked like it had been cauterized."

"What do you mean, *cauterized*?"

"Burned. Scarred. Like something had sealed it over so it wouldn't bleed."

Zack hesitated, then decided what he wanted to say. "When you can, tell Dad I found what he wanted me to."

"What?"

"Just say I found it. It'll cheer him up."

"I'll tell him." His mother gave him the phone number of the hospital. "You take care," she said. "Water the plants. Lock the doors. And try not to make a mess of the house, all right, honey?"

"Sure."

"Good night, dear."

"Night, Mom," Zack said, and hung up the phone. He went back into the living room. "Everything's okay," he told Uta. "I didn't tell her about Honker because she'd go bonkers."

"I know what you mean." Uta checked the time. "It's getting late," she said. "I guess you should give me a lift home. My folks won't worry about me. They know I can take care of myself—but you don't want to be out driving too late."

CLUNK.

A noise outside.

"What's that?" Uta asked.

"Skunks and raccoons have been raiding the garbage cans," Zack said.

He checked out a side window. The garbage cans in the breezeway were upright with their lids on. A wind rustled the leaves of the trees and whipped tumbleweed toward the cattle pond. Honker sniffed at the air. Picasso growled.

Uta reached out to pet Picasso. "They hear something."

"It's nothing," Zack said, coming back to sit on the sofa.

CLUNK. CLUNK.

"That's no skunk," Uta said. She got up and pulled open the drapes covering the glass sliding doors of the living room. The outside patio was a maze of shadows.

Nothing moved.

She turned away from the slabs of glass and sat in one of the rattan chairs. Zack slid to the floor next to Honker and started talking to him. "She wants me to bring you back to the cave—you believe that?"

"Look, even if he *is* a real, living dinosaur—which I still don't completely believe—you've got a responsibility . . ."

CLUNK. CLUNK. CLUNK.

"What if that's his mother now, Mr. Egg Man?" Uta added.

Zack laughed. "Mothers don't go running around all over looking for their eggs."

"I wouldn't underestimate what any mother would do," Uta said. "My uncle knew a man who found a bear cub and brought it back to his trailer. He was going to sell it to a zoo in San Diego—but the mother bear came down from the mountains, tore the door off his trailer, and started chewing on the man. She took her baby back and ran off with the man's arm in her mouth."

"We're not talking bears."

"Well, it's the same thing. You don't find a fantastic

creature like a baby dinosaur, and say, 'Oh, I think I'll keep it so my dad can be famous and make a few bucks!' You'd be a jerk."

"My father only took this job because he needed the money. That's the only reason he agreed to live in this wasteland." The words had spilled out before he could stop them.

"Wasteland! This is not a wasteland," Uta said. "You just don't like it because it's not wall-to-wall malls and surfing bimbos and amusement parks like L.A. All I'm saying is that you've got to realize you've found something that's very important. Something priceless."

"I sure hope so."

Uta's face turned red and she put her hands on her hips. "Don't you understand? There are dinosaurs; maybe a bunch of them—a herd!—has survived somewhere in Silver Mountain! And one of their babies is right here in this room with us! Can't you realize what that means?"

"Yeah, I realize what it means," Zack said, laughing. "A truck full of money!"

The sounds were at the front door now.

SCRATCH.

SCRAAAAATCH.

ATTACK

*P*icasso got up, dropped his bone, and froze, staring at the front door. The scraping sounds were quieter, but closer. So close they seemed to be coming from inside the house.

Quietly, Zack got up from the sofa. When he reached the hallway, he heard a *creak*. Slowly, the front door bent in, its thick brass hinges straining under the pressure. He tiptoed to the door, silently set the dead-bolt lock, and peered out through the peephole.

Nothing but blackness.

Creeeaaak.

The door pressed in again as a low beastly growl began to shake the floorboards. A stench of rot filled his nostrils, and for the first time in a long, long time, Zack was scared. The chain lock rattled in his hand as he hooked it in place. He was aware Uta was standing right behind him.

"What is it?" Uta whispered.

"Something big. *Real big.*"

Zack looked back through the peephole. He saw an enormous silhouette backlighted by a bulb burning in the breezeway. A moment more, and the massive shape blocked everything from view. "No rhinos in Utah, right?" he joked nervously.

SCRATCH. SCRAAAATCH.

"Get away from the door," Uta said. She backed up into the living room, taking Honker and Picasso with her.

Zack eased the palm of his hand against the door. He felt a vibration, a movement, as though something sharp was being drawn slowly back and forth across the door. The motion became faster, like the way Picasso would scratch the bottom of the door when he wanted to come in.

"Don't," Uta warned Zack, as he pressed his ear against the door.

Suddenly, there was a roar, and a single claw punched through the door, just inches from Zack's face. The roar rose in volume and pitch, topping out into a chilling, junglelike scream. Combined with Uta's shriek, it pained Zack's ears.

Zack realized that he, too, was screaming.

Within a moment, the entire door was torn away and

in the doorway loomed the immense mother raptor. Zack was paralyzed at the sight. The upper ridges of her skull were pronounced like a gorilla's—thrusts of brow overhanging hugely swollen and yellow eyes. Her teeth were bared, thick jagged points that meshed perfectly into a hideous smile. A dark band ran from her head down to the tip of her thick, rigid tail.

Zack stared into her huge, freakish eyes as they swung like radar discs in deep glistening sockets. They stopped—riveted on him.

ROARRRR.

The mother raptor's jaws shot forward, a blur of teeth biting into what was left of the door frame. Zack's mind spun madly. He was barely aware that Uta was shouting at him. He heard Picasso barking, and he remembered the hatchling. He turned and ran down the hallway toward the kitchen.

The mother raptor saw the motion and took a single rapid leap after him. Her tail swung, skittering a hat rack across the floor. The smells of the house stunned her. She sniffed frantically at the new terrain, then continued deliberately after Zack. Her body listed and smashed against the walls, knocking a row of framed photos to the floor.

Zack glanced over his shoulder as he ran. He saw the

long snout of the raptor striking out ferociously, snapping at him like the beak of a great, monstrous hawk. Folds of loose, dead skin on the giant lizard's neck fluttered as her jaws chomped at the air. Zack flicked light switches off as he ran, searching madly for pockets of darkness, anything that could hide him.

Anything to let him escape.

One of the raptor's claws slammed into the wall behind him, tearing off a strip of molding. Zack saw the raptor's eyes clearly now, huge glaring bubbles larger than raptor's eyes in any paleontologist's sketch. The dinosaur's absurdly small forearms were rippled with muscles. They flailed at Zack, claws whooshing through the air. A single sickle-sized claw on each of its thick hind limbs tore into the rug runner, shredding it like paper.

Zack's chest heaved painfully. He spun away from the bright lights of the kitchen and made a sharp turn into the darkness of his parents' bedroom. Dark was safe, he thought. She wouldn't see him in the darkness.

The raptor turned into the room after him. Too late, Zack realized he had backed himself into a corner without windows.

Nowhere to run! He pressed against a wall to hide behind the end of a heavy oak bureau. The mother raptor stopped at the foot of the bed. She reared herself up, her head scraping the ceiling. There was a spill of light from the doorway, and Zack saw her deadly anatomy. Her forelimbs dangled in front of her now, both ending in four gnarled, thick fingers tipped by claws the size of a grizzly's. Each foot had three large, thick spikes pointing straight forward—with a fourth longer, more terrible claw arching up from the ankle.

The raptor's nostrils quivered. She sensed Zack hiding in the shadows. Roaring, she lurched forward, swinging her forelimbs out at him. A claw hooked into the bureau, and she hurled all of it, its drawers and mirror and stacked clothing, through the air. Zack leaped across the bed, but the raptor was fast after him. He tripped on a bedpost. As he fell the raptor's arm swished below him like a samurai's blade.

ROAR.

Zack felt a stabbing pain as his head bashed into the corner of an end table. He felt something trickling down his face and into his eyes. He wiped at it. Blood.

His blood.

The raptor turned. Its tail ripped through his mother's lotions bottles and crushed a white wicker desk. Zack tried to stand, but he was dazed. He looked up into the gaping jaws of the mother raptor. His body began to shake with terror as he reached out into the shadows, his

45 MAYVILLE PUBLIC LIBRARY
MAYVILLE, NORTH DAKOTA
-18,230-

fingers searching for a shoetree or a loose hanger.

A weapon.

Anything.

Zack's lungs filled with the wet, stinking graveyard breath of the raptor. Hot yellow froth drooled down onto him from the spray of ginzu fangs that jutted out from the raptor's gums. The buzzardlike fingers of her forearms seized him, began to lift him up. Her tongue slithered from between her fangs. It crawled over his face, its slimy and scalding strip writhing down his brow toward his chin.

The forearms squeezed him, pressed the breath half out of him. Gnarled fingers welted his skin, and he could barely think. *What are you doing?* He wanted to ask. *What's happening? What?* The raptor's thick rough tongue halted on Zack's lips and began to force down his chin and creep into his mouth.

"NOOOOOO!" Zack screamed. He tasted the slippery tip of the tongue as it crept through his lips and down his throat. Its rancid froth and ooze reeked with the rot of death, and he began to gag, to feel his own vomit moving up to greet the pulsing, wet slime.

Somewhere in his clouded mind he heard something. Noises. *Sounds coming from behind the raptor.*

The mother raptor dropped Zack, and he glimpsed

Uta shouting in the doorway of the bedroom. Picasso barked and growled ferociously, and nipped at the dinosaur's heels. Honker scooted up to Picasso's side and joined in sounding the outrage. The hatchling hadn't the faintest idea it was scolding his own half-ton mother.

The giant raptor turned from Zack toward the shrieking trio.

ROARRRRR.

The entire bedroom shook like an earthquake. The raptor lunged toward Uta. She went silent, backed up, and took off toward the living room, Picasso along with her.

Honker held his ground, hissing fiercely.

The mother raptor cocked her head and looked curiously down at the hatchling. She lowered her snout and slowly extended her stinking, slimy tongue toward her offspring. Honker glared at the giant creature. For a moment he spun like a dazed chicken, then understood that this monstrosity wanted *him*.

He turned and fled.

ROAR.

The raptor took off after Honker. She closed on him, but he made a sudden turn out the gutted shell of what once was the front doorway. The mother raptor raced out after him, roaring into the night.

Zack wiped the raptor's slime and froth from his lips

and patted at the clot forming on his forehead. He staggered back down the hallway to the living room. He had seen the raptor leave, but knew she could return at any moment. He spotted Uta crouched behind the sofa. "Come on," he called to her—and she came running.

Zack led the way down a back hallway, with Picasso trailing. It was narrower and darker. It would be more difficult for the raptor to follow them. He herded everyone into a shadowy bathroom and slammed the door. Uta looked around at the cramped little room with its shower tub and cinder-block walls. "Great," she said. "Now we're *really* trapped."

"It doesn't want us," Zack said. "Besides, you haven't lived until you've been sloppy-kissed by a raptor!"

"You're going to make me throw up."

"Shhh. Quiet."

Zack slid his back down against a tiled wall until he was sitting on the floor. Uta sat down next to him. "D'you hear that?" she asked as she petted Picasso, keeping one hand curled around his snout in case she had to muzzle him.

"What?" Zack asked.

"*That.*"

He listened. After a moment, he heard what sounded like the whistle of a distant teakettle. It grew louder. Closer.

Uta gasped. "The window!" Zack shifted forward onto his knees. He slid open the shower doors mounted on the tub. Reflected light from the breezeway bounced off a small, *open* window.

There was the sound of scurrying, like a small animal was running through the gravel and wood chips of the back garden. Something spooked and shuddering flew up onto the windowsill. Zack thought it was a cat.

Uta screeched. "Oh, God, it's Honker! Get him out of here! Out!"

"Too late," Zack said, slamming the window closed and locking it.

"What do you mean, *too late*?"

Zack cradled Honker in his arms. "He's shaking."

"So what?"

"It's okay, little fella. It's okay. . . ." Honker started to nuzzle into Zack's lap. He honked gratefully and then began to rub heads with Picasso.

"He missed Picasso," Zack whispered.

Uta looked at Zack like he was insane. "Get him out of here! The mother wants him! You said it yourself!"

"Hey, he's scared."

"Who isn't?"

"She'll eat him."

"No, she won't." Uta slammed the shower doors

closed. "You don't seem to realize that *we're* the only ones on the menu tonight!"

Zack put his a finger up to his lips. "Shhh."

For a while there were no sounds.

"Is she gone?" Uta whispered.

The silence went on.

"She must have gotten tired of looking," Zack said. They began to relax and breathe again.

CRAAAASH.

The mother's head exploded through the window like a battering ram. She roared at them, with only the glass of the shower doors between her and them. She swung her jaws the length of the tub. The tip of each fang was chalk white, a light yellow film coating the shank, with a sludge of green rot on the gum line. Remnants of the decaying otters were wedged between the teeth, sinews of the carcasses dropping upon the glass like bleached worms. There were maggots in her nose.

The mother raptor looked directly at the cowering foursome. She shot a single hind leg up onto what remained of the windowsill. She thrust down hard, and one of her razor-sharp claws sliced through the wall. Strips of metal siding and tile fell away, leaving a gaping hole.

Shaking violently, the raptor shimmied the whole of

her body in at them, her forelimbs clawing at the shower doors. The aluminum frames bent until the glass pinioned the four of them like butterflies.

ROARRR.

The mother raptor slid her snout along the surface of the glass until her jaws were over Zack's face. She snapped at the glass, puzzled why she couldn't taste flesh. She swung her jaws directly to Uta.

"How can it see us in the dark?" Zack yelled.

"Look at her eyes?" Uta screamed. "Things in caves grow fat eyes. They can see fine in the dark!" Her gaze shot up the shadows of the wall as the mother raptor pounded ferociously on the glass. The slabs began to shatter, squiggly cracks radiating out from each impact. Picasso yelped. Honker shrieked. Zack saw Uta pointing to the light switch high on the wall.

"Put the lights on!" Uta yelled. *"ON!"*

Zack realized she was right. He began waving beneath the glass to distract the raptor. She swung her head to look at him, then slammed her claws relentlessly down onto the glass.

BLAM! BLAM! BLAM!

One of the slabs shattered. Zack pushed up hard on a large piece of jagged glass. He rose into a crouch. Using the slab as a shield, he pushed it into the raptor's face, reached out, and hit the wall switch. A ceiling bank of fluorescent lights burst into blazing strips of brilliance. The raptor swung her gaze upward, her bulbous eyes wide open. She roared with pain and reared as her fore-limbs flailed in vain to bring back the darkness.

"Come on!" Zack shouted to Uta.

He gave the wedge of glass a final thrust, allowing Uta to scramble out from under it, with Picasso and Honker right after her. When they were clear, he let go and started out the doorway. *Crash!* The raptor shattered the lights, tubes bursting and raining sparks onto the tile floor. She saw the motion now, lurched, and struck out at it. A claw caught Zack's shirt and he cried out.

Uta saw what was happening and turned back. She grabbed Zack's hand, pulling him after her. His shirt ripped free from the claw, and they dashed back down the hall. Another tube burst, showering glass and fluores-cent powder into the raptor's eyes.

ROAR.

ROAAAR.

Uta turned to flee out the front of the house. "No!" Zack shouted. "We wouldn't stand a chance out there!" He yanked her after him into the living room and dragged a halogen floor lamp to the far wall. A row of track lights hung from one of the beams. "Grab all the lamps you can!"

Uta seized a lamp from a table near the sofa and set it into the cluster of lights. Picasso began to chase his own tail. The trembling form of the hatchling stayed by Zack as the roars of the mother raptor became louder.

Closer.

They had every lamp in the room bunched together. "Get behind the lights!" Zack said, flicking on all the switches. Uta grabbed the poker from the fireplace. She reached it up to the blazing track lights and focused them toward the black hole at the end of the hallway.

CRASH.

More glass shattering.

The mother raptor, bruised and cut, emerged roaring from the hall. Her tongue shot out to lick at the blood oozing from gashes on her shoulders. She stared at the wall of lights.

"She can't see us," Zack said.

A chill slid down Uta's spine. She began to pray that something magical would happen. Something crazy, like the Great Spirit would appear and turn the raptor to stone. She squeezed Zack's hand. Picasso was silent. Honker made short, terrified sounds.

"Give him up or we're dead!" Uta hissed.

"No."

The mother raptor lowered her head. Her jutting brow shaded her eyes, and she started toward them.

"Oh, God," Zack said. Crazy ideas began to race through his mind. He thought of throwing a lamp and trying to electrocute the mother raptor. He saw the TV remote on a table next to Uta.

"Turn the TV on! Turn it on!" he shouted.

Uta saw the control, picked it up, and pressed the power button. Behind the raptor, a platinum-haired weather woman came on the TV screen, her voice blaring about a coming storm.

The mother raptor halted. She looked at the TV and let out a roar. Zack couldn't get Honker to be quiet. He saw the intercom in the wall behind him, turned it on, and lifted Honker's squawking mouth up toward the mike. With a twist of the volume dial, Honker's cries came out of speakers all over the house.

ROAR.

The mother raptor turned in confusion. She looked toward the hall, then back to the TV. She took a leap away from the blazing assembly of lights, but then turned suddenly, like a monstrous bird of prey.

Uta gasped. "I think we went too far."

The raptor charged up to the burning lights. She was close enough for Zack and Uta to see the wet fungus and lice that festered on her snout. Now, her eyes locked on Honker.

ROAR.

She spun. Her tail, with a single sweep, knocked out half of the halogen lights. Bulbs exploded, and the raptor thrust her jaws forward. Uta screamed. She struck at the window behind them with the poker. Honker shuddered and leaped out of Zack's arms. He ran along the floor, trembling as the mother raptor's jaws swooped downward.

"Don't!" Zack shouted.

The jaws of the raptor closed on Honker. Zack thought the hatchling was being devoured alive. The mother flipped Honker, positioned him in her mouth as she retreated with her prize.

"Let him go," Zack yelled. His shins slammed into an overturned table and he fell. By the time he was on his feet, the mother raptor had fled out the hole where the front door had been.

Zack limped outside into the light of the breezeway, with Uta and Picasso fast behind. Beyond the circle of light, they saw the dark shadow of Silver Mountain as the roaring of the mother raptor and faint shrieks of Honker faded into the night.

SPIDER GRANDMA

Zack ran after the sounds for several hundred feet, beyond a paddock and up a hillside until he was surrounded by night and the pounding of his heart. Uta and Picasso ran after him. Uta took his hand and made him turn back. Inside the house, she had him stand under the kitchen light. The cut on his forehead had stopped bleeding, but it was swollen.

"Are you okay?" Uta asked.

"Yes," Zack said.

Uta grabbed a handful of ice cubes from the refrigerator and wrapped them in a dish towel. She pressed the towel gently on the cut. "We're lucky we're not dead, you know."

"What about Honker?" Zack asked. "Maybe he wasn't so lucky."

"You never should have taken that egg. That's the first rule about wilderness—leave wildlife alone!"

"He's probably been devoured by now."

"Hey, I've seen a lot of lizards in the desert. They're not cannibals."

"These are dinosaurs!" Zack said.

"So? Honker's with his mother," Uta said. "They wouldn't have survived this long if they didn't protect their young. That's all she was doing, you know—protecting him."

Zack took the compress and pressed it harder on the small wound. "Well, then he's in that mountain somewhere, and I want to see where!"

"Why?"

"There's got to be more of them, you know! There could be all kinds of weird stuff going on in there!"

"Great. Freak Mountain."

"Right. There could be time mutants all over the place!"

"You're going after him, aren't you?" Uta asked in disbelief.

"Yeah, so?"

"So, you're crazy."

"Didn't you like Honker?"

"Sure. I had a pet skunk once, too. And I liked him. I

like all animals. But I wouldn't want to die for one."

"Honker imprinted on me," Zack said. "Besides, he's cool. And he doesn't deserve that nasty biological mother he's got!"

"Hey, she came all the way back for him, you know."

"Oh, I know, all right." Zack tossed the compress into the garbage and headed down the hallway.

Uta followed and spoke softly. "You and Picasso can't stay here tonight." She brushed her fingers through her hair, sweeping out specks of plaster. "We've got to tell somebody what happened. Maybe we should contact Dr. Bones."

"No way." Zack opened a closet and grabbed a hammer and nails from a tool kit. "My dad found the egg. *We* were almost eaten alive. We tell Bones *nothing*!"

Uta and Picasso followed Zack out to the front of the house. He picked up the remnants of the front door and began to hammer planks, crisscrossing them over the entrance.

"You going to call your dad?" Uta asked.

"Not tonight. He's too sick."

"Then tell your mom."

"She'd call a shrink. You don't tell anyone on the phone that you've found a dinosaur. Nobody'll believe us. Nobody!" They used a few old sheets of plywood to patch up the other windows.

Later, exhausted, Zack stood frozen in the light of the breezeway. He reached down and picked up Picasso. "My father's dino is in that mountain," Zack said. "You don't know, really, what this would mean for him. I'm not going to let it disappear. My dad didn't get hurt for nothing!"

"Well, that baby dinosaur has rights, too." Uta saw Zack's eyes were glistening. "Right now, we've got to get out of here," she said gently. Uta headed for the motorcycle. "I'll hold Picasso if you drive slowly."

"It's okay," Zack said. "He's got his own wheels." He went to a storage shed and came back pulling a tiny trailer with bicycle wheels. It looked like a miniature trotting rig.

Uta laughed. "I should have known you'd have invented something."

"Hey, he loves it," Zack said, hitching the trailer to the back of the motorcycle. He put Picasso into his safety harness, then climbed on and kick-started the engine. The headlight cut into the night as Uta swung up behind him.

"Where to?" Zack asked.

"I want to stop by my house," Uta said. "My folks and Larry Ghost Coyote'll want to know we're back from the mountain. Then we'll go visit somebody."

"Who?"

"Spider Grandma."

"Spider who?"

"She's my grandmother. You'll like her. She's the one with the turquoise concession and tents on the road to Altamont. The one with pinwheels and reflectors, and the big neon sign that flashes FIREWORKS! She's got old maps of Silver Mountain and the caves. Lots of stuff. We can trust her and she'll know what we should do."

Dr. Boneid had another nip of cognac from his small silver flask. He revved the engine, and his Range Rover rolled away from Doc Morrison's ranch. The headlights bounced off a patch of thick night fog that rolled off the river.

Another small swig.

Boneid let the alcohol roll from one side of his mouth to the other, gave it time to release its bouquet—then swallowed slowly so it could soothe his throat. His house call to Dr. Morrison's had finished the day's damage control. He had watched and guided the old doctor as he filled out Norak's medical report. He had the foresight to dictate an addendum for the doctor. The report would make it clear the accident had happened outside the dig perimeter—and that no university equipment was in use when Professor Norak took his little tumble.

Now there was no way Norak could sue anyone, even if he was crippled for life.

Boneid chuckled and continued driving down the long, steep, rocky way that Morrison called his driveway. *Can't you pave it, you cheap quack!*

The fog surrounded him as the road dipped across a dried riverbed strewn with large, jagged rocks. He switched to the amber fog lights, and turned on his wipers as the windshield beaded with moisture. Proceeding at a crawl, he hunched forward between the *flick, flick* of the wipers.

Near the main highway, the fog began to lift. He put the pedal down to make some time as he leaned his head back for another sip from the flask. This would be his last for the night, he thought. He knew a few of the other jealous professors on the university staff had begun whispering about him.

He's begun to drink. He's a raving, slobbering alcoholic.

But Boneid knew he wasn't. He could stop anytime he wanted. But if anything would drive a man to drink, it was northwest Utah.

Smoke rose from the desert gravel as Boneid slammed on the brakes. He looked out the windshield, and the flask fell from his hand. He didn't notice it emptying itself on his lap. All he thought was that he *was* losing his mind. There, out of the mist and the darkness, came something that bad dreams are made of.

Something astonishing.

Terrifying.

Yes, he had been drinking. True, he was exhausted. But even in all of his darkest dreams and those lost gambling weekends, he could never have imagined the creature that dashed across the road in front of the Rover. It had turned to look at him. A monstrous lizard with saber teeth and a long tongue. There was a blur, then it roared and opened its mouth. In there, sitting on its tongue was a juvenile, a baby creature, thrashing, looking as though it were trying to shake itself loose.

Then, just as quickly, the monstrosity disappeared into a wisp of fog.

Boneid punched the glove compartment latch. Its door sprung open and he grabbed a pistol. He raced out of the Rover and into the fog after the creature. He ran through one sliver of fog and into another, his feet tripping on moonstones the size of his fist.

Finally, he fell and his pistol flew from his hands. He began to crawl about searching for it, when he heard a roar and felt the earth shaking beneath him. He managed to stand as the fog cleared. He saw the huge creature bounding straight at him. "Oh, God," he cried out. He turned and began to run back toward the Rover. He stumbled and fell again. He got up and kept running.

The fog grew thick again, but off to his left—where he wasn't expecting it—were the blazing headlights and ghostly shape of the Rover. The roaring behind him was louder now. He threw his mind free of alcohol. Adrenaline charged his heart until his chest and brain hurt.

He reached the Rover, threw open the door and leaped inside. The creature's gnarled and glistening snout exploded from the fog. The smaller, squirming lizard in its mouth dropped to the ground and scurried off. Now the creature's hideous head was smack against the driver's window, its eyes peering in at him.

Boneid punched wildly at the horn, blasting it again and again as he tried to start the Rover.

CRASH.

The mother raptor's head shattered the window. Boneid threw himself toward the passenger door. He smelled the stench hissing from the creature's mouth as it released its jaw adductor muscles—widening its mouth! Its jaws snapped savagely, nearly engulfing the steering wheel. Boneid's body shook convulsively, his jacket caught on the green-rot-covered base of one of the raptor's fangs. The creature's tongue slid up around Boneid's neck, as his free hand struggled to reach the small, round button of the cigarette lighter. Finally, it popped and Boneid grabbed it. He thrust the hot, burning coils of the cigarette lighter down onto the raptor's tongue. There was the sound of sizzling.

A burning.

The raptor shrieked and snapped its head back reflexively. Boneid's arm was freed and his hand shot to the ignition key. The Rover started and he threw it into gear—smashing his foot down onto the gas pedal. The tires screamed as they spun in the sand of the dry river bottom. The creature slammed its forelimbs down onto the roof of the car. Its claws ripped through the metal and leather as the tires began to grip, and the Rover lurched forward.

ROAR.

The creature let loose its grip and ran alongside, biting off the protruding side mirror. Its gargantuan head loomed outside Boneid's window again. He saw the shreds of death dripping from its teeth—the ghastly eyes filled with unspeakable rage!

The Rover picked up speed, but not before the creature let loose a stream of spittle from its mouth. Green and steaming fluids hit the hood, washing over it like vomit with chunks and shreds of half-digested prey. Boneid watched as the vomit began to coat the hood and dry into gossamer, weblike strands.

But he was traveling fast now—out of the fog and onto the main road. He was riveted on the rearview mirror, watching the creature disappear back into the fog. He floored the Rover completely now, brought it up to seventy, then eighty miles an hour. Already he was thinking about which of his men he could tell about what he'd seen. A living raptor! A *Utahraptor*! The largest and most terrifying of all the predators that had ever lived.

Beyond *T. rex*.

Beyond sanity.

Boneid would need help for the tracking. The hunt. He would find the creature if it took the rest of his life and every penny of the university to do it. He'd need men he could depend upon, workers he could trust. He knew not many would believe he had seen a creature that seemed to stare into his very soul.

Zack turned the motorcycle off the dirt road and onto the paved highway. When they reached Uta's house, he stopped and she jumped off and ran inside. Zack kept the engine running and let Picasso out of the cart for a run. He'd met her parents a few times when he and Uta were working on their science project. They were very traditional Utes, but modern enough to have a big-screen TV and a good sound system. They also seemed to trust Uta and let her do just about anything she wanted.

Uta came back out, and he put Picasso into his trailer. They headed west for several miles on Altamont Road, as far as the FIREWORKS! sign.

"Spider Grandma keeps her stand open late," Uta said. "She doesn't want to miss any passing tourists."

Zack parked between a pay phone booth and a hanging wall of bright-colored Ute rugs and blankets that undulated in the wind. He put Picasso on his leash and walked with him by phosphorescent paintings on velvet, Day-Glo images of flying geese, cougars, and bear designs. An old woman hobbled toward them through a maze of swinging purple lightbulbs and bug zappers.

"Hello, Spider Grandma," Uta said.

A mouth in the wrinkled cracked face opened and a strong, perky voice erupted. "Hello yourself, Uta. Long time, no see."

"I'm sorry," Uta said. "I've been busy. This is Zack, Spider Grandma. I wanted him to meet you because we have to talk."

The bright yellow of the neon sign struck the old woman's face from the side. Zack was startled by the leathery, deep wrinkles. Her hair was cut short like a 1920s dancing girl, and she wore bear-claw earrings and a shawl over a flowery housecoat.

"Hello, Zack," Spider Grandma said. "Nice little poodle you've got there."

"Thanks."

She leaned down to run her fingers through Picasso's white shaggy hair, but he barked.

"Sorry," Zack said.

"That's all right. I love *barking* dogs, too. What can I do for you?" Spider Grandma asked. "You and Picasso want to buy something?"

"No, thanks," Zack said.

"Shame. Everyone who comes to my stand must buy something or they have a lifetime of bad luck and never find what they're looking for."

"In that case, what can I get for five bucks?" Zack asked.

"Bingo," Spider Grandma said. "That's enough for a nice quartz crystal or a couple of dozen night crawlers, if you're a fisherman. It's enough for lots of things."

Zack dug into the pocket of his jeans, pulled out a five-dollar bill, and handed it over to Spider Grandma. "Fine," she said. "Now you will have excellent luck. What do you want? A clay pipe? An eagle tie clip?"

"Do you have any arrowheads?"

"Oh, do I!" Spider Grandma took his arm and led him around the stand to a table covered with plastic containers filled with minerals, fossils, and other souvenirs. Zack poured through one container and picked out a pointed, scallop-edged arrowhead. "I'll take this one."

"Fine," Spider Grandma said. "Shall I wrap it?"

"No, thanks," Zack said, putting it into his back pocket.

"Now we can talk," Spider Grandma said, heading for a wrought-iron table with chairs set up near a grill. She motioned for Zack and Uta to sit with her as she grabbed a leg from a baked chicken sitting in a Pyrex dish. "You kids hungry?"

"No, thanks," Zack said. Picasso began to beg so Zack picked him up and sat down with him on his lap. Uta slid into a chair next to Spider Grandma and began to pick at a few roasted carrots that lay in the juices of the baking dish.

From out of the blue, Spider Grandma said, "I hope no one died a terrible death." She ripped off pieces of fat from the chicken and fed them to Picasso.

"No," Zack said, surprised. "What made you ask that?"

"Because I was here last week," she said, "taking inventory, when a wind came up. I had a vision that someone died a bizarre and painful death. It was as if I could feel it. A painful death floating on the wind."

"No one died that we know of," Uta said. "We're here because we *saw* something."

"Something near Silver Mountain," Zack added.

"What?"

Zack cleared his throat. "It looked like a dinosaur." He kept his eyes on the old woman, watching for her reaction. "We wondered if you had ever heard of any dinosaurs around here? Living dinosaurs."

"*Living* dinosaurs?"

"Yes," Uta said.

"You can let your dog run," Spider Grandma told Zack. "I can see he's a good boy." She turned the carcass of the chicken over and began to pick away at the small, tender pockets of meat on its underside. "Zack, you're a city boy, aren't you? You have the spirit of Rollerblades, surfboards, and swimming pools. Not the spirit of the wolf, like the Utes."

"Spider Grandma," Uta said. "You know I have the spirit of the wolf, and *I* saw the dinosaur, too. It's very big, and it's very real." She put her arm around her grandmother. "And Zack knows his dinosaurs. His father's a paleontologist on the university dig. We saw a giant *Utahraptor*."

Spider Grandma tore open a Handi-Wipe and started

cleaning her hands. "Well, then, you've both seen proof of dragons," she said. "That's what some of the folks around here call dinosaurs. There are as many legends about the dinosaurs here as there are bones."

"Did anyone besides us ever tell you they've seen a living dinosaur?" Zack asked. "Anyone, *ever.*"

Uta's grandmother said, "There are some men who have gotten lost in the mine shafts and caves of Silver Mountain. There are seventy miles of shafts and tunnels, and hundreds of caves, some of them as big as your churches. There are sacred drawings on the walls. Rock paintings, petroglyphs of demons and mysterious horned figures. Some of the old miners told me stories about seeing very large creatures. Usually, it was after they'd had a few drinks.

"They'd come to me for herbs. I was like a Florence Nightingale and Kmart to them. I sold them beer and chocolates and cigarettes, too. Some of the men who worked in the mountain disappeared and never came out. Some thought there was disease in the guano, the crap from bats and birds that piles up in the caves. A few men breathed the dust from the guano and died of rabies. A lot of people think you have to be bitten, but that's not true. One inspector said there were also pockets of methane and carbon monoxide that made men hallucinate. Some people heard screams in the mountain. But what do you care? Why don't you just forget about it?"

"A real live dino isn't something I want to forget about. Especially, when it's imprinted on me and its mother destroyed half our house!"

The old woman looked to see what was in Uta's eyes.

"I told him he's crazy to go back there," Uta said. "You should have seen that mother dinosaur! It was horrible. It almost killed us! But he insists that he's got to find the little one. So I told him we could trust you and that you have maps."

"I see," Spider Grandma said. "That I have maps is true."

"Could you give me one?" Zack asked. "A map that would show me the safest way into and out of the mountain."

"All the maps I have are in Ute," Spider Grandma said. She looked to Uta. "He doesn't know our language."

Uta saw Zack's eyes beginning to glisten again. She knew he was thinking of his father. "I'm going with him," she said.

"No, Uta," he said. "You stay and take care of Picasso for me."

"I'm going."

"No, you're not."

"Yes, I am."

"Stop bellyaching," Spider Grandma scolded, sitting back down at the table. "I believe there are horrible beasts lurking in the darkness of the caves. Even if you managed to stay clear of the beasts, you'd still have to eat." She leaned closer to Zack. "A city boy like you would lose his way and starve to death."

"No, I wouldn't. I'd eat roots."

"Caves don't have a lot of roots," Uta said. "Besides, half of them are poisonous or would give you the runs."

"She's right," Spider Grandma said. "The only people who survive are those who can eat the grubs that live in the cave mud." She reached out and clamped a hand on Zack's shoulder. "Could you eat grubs?"

"Sure," Zack said. "What are they?"

"Larvae." Spider Grandma wiped her hands on the tablecloth, got up, and went to a Styrofoam bait cooler. She lifted out a tray, took the lid off of it, and brought it to Zack. "These are the Silver Mountain grubs," she said. "Fishermen buy them to catch smallmouth river bass."

Zack felt his stomach roll, then twist as he peered into the container. Its surface was a bed of plump, squirming, worms. They were white, glistening in their own shiny mucus.

"They're pukey," Zack said.

"Not when you have the spirit of the wolf inside you

and are hungry," Spider Grandma said, stirring the twitching mass of larvae with her finger. "Uta could eat a grub, couldn't you, dear? All my grandchildren can eat grubs."

"Can't you just show me a safe path into the mountain? I could rescue this baby dinosaur," Zack told the old woman. "His name's Honker. He's almost like a pet. My father found it. It belongs to him."

"No, that's where you're wrong," Spider Grandma said. "No living creature belongs to anyone. All animals are our equals in this world. They have wisdom to share with humans, and you should know that."

"I tried to tell him," Uta said.

"Besides, you'd get lost and starve to death unless you could eat grubs," Spider Grandma said. "They don't have quarter-pound hamburgers and chocolate shakes where you want to go."

Zack cleared his throat. "I could eat a grub if I had to."

"No, L.A. Boy. You would die without your fajitas."

"If I ate a grub now, right this minute, would that prove I'm serious?"

Spider Grandma studied his face closely. "Yes," she said. "That would show me that you are very serious."

"Then give me one."

"You got it." Spider Grandma stuck her hand into the

squirming mass and pulled out a big fat grub. It was nearly three inches long and over an inch through the middle. Strands of slime clung to it like melted cheese. "Would you like it roasted?"

"Yes," Uta answered for Zack. Picasso watched curiously.

"Forgive me," Spider Grandma muttered as she dropped the grub onto the embers of the fire. It began to twist and turn. A yellow flame rose and licked at it. Its coat of mucus began to singe. A second longer, and Spider Grandma scooped the larva out of the fire with a large metal spoon. It was still moving.

"Take it," Spider Grandma ordered Zack.

Slowly, Zack grasped the grub between his fingers. The heat of the fire had caused it to swell, and he felt riblike bumps encircling its body.

"Do it!" Uta said.

Zack popped the grub into his mouth. He felt it squirming in the saliva on his tongue. At first, he thought his stomach was going to fly out of him, but he worked the grub to one side of his mouth. He hesitated a moment longer, then quickly bit down. The grub exploded like a liquid-filled candy, one of those small wax candies that burst with sugary water when you bite it. Part of the fluids from the grub burst out and leaked down his chin. He wiped at his lips, and swallowed quickly. The body of the grub slid down his throat like a living, wiggling wad of fat.

"Nice," Spider Grandma said. "You ate the grub. I personally think a good grub's got more vitamins than a burger. Still, I don't think you should go to the mountain. It would be foolish."

"I'm going anyway," Zack said. He wiped at his mouth and picked at a few last shreds of grub that were stuck between his teeth.

"I see," Spider Grandma said. "And you, Uta. Are you still going with him?" She watched her granddaughter look to Zack. Spider Grandma saw her catch her breath.

Uta answered softly, "Yes, Grandma."

Spider Grandma sighed and sent her thoughts skyward searching for a vision. All that came was a memory of herself when she was Uta's age. She remembered a brave as handsome as Zack trying to impress her with long braids and dancing in skins of bears and buffalo.

Spider Grandma smiled at Uta. "I see you know what you must do." She went to a rusty file cabinet standing in the corner of the tent. She turned back to them holding a copy of a map. "The copy machine I use is crummy, but this will show you the safest entrance and a good route up through the mountain."

Zack took the map and opened it. The old woman pointed to its markings. "It will show you what springs you may drink from, which roots and mushrooms *not* to eat, and most of the quicksand pits and weakened shafts." She pointed to several clumps of *XXX*s. "These show the location of petroglyphs. When in doubt, you must follow the rock paintings of rising ropes and flute players. They look like snake charmers. Ignore the paintings of demons, or they will lead you down to death. Do you understand?"

"Yes, Spider Grandma," Zack said.

Uta nodded.

"Good," Spider Grandma said. She put the map in a plastic bag and gave it to Zack. "This will keep the map dry. And, there is one thing more you will need to make the journey safely." She stood up, pulled the belt of her housedress tight, and signaled them to follow her into a smaller tent near the corral.

"I knew she'd give us a special charm," Uta whispered.

Spider Grandma overheard her. "You're right," she said. "I like you both very much. It's not every day my granddaughter and her friend come in here and tell me they've seen a living dinosaur. The two of you may be a little kooky, but I think you both have the spirit of the wolf. Still, you will need a very powerful talisman." She stopped before an old, battered cabinet, stooped down, and lifted up what looked like a human skull.

"Is that skull *real*?" Zack asked.

"It depends on whether someone is going to buy it or not," Spider Grandma said. She lifted off the top of the skull like it was the lid of a cookie jar. Inside was a shiny black cell phone. She handed it to Zack. "I will lend you my cell phone. I keep it hidden from my workers. They're always trying to call Mexico."

Suddenly, there was a flash of light.

BAM.

A thunderbolt came from out of nowhere and struck a tall, lone pine on the hillside. The wind picked up fast, snapping the lines of the hanging blankets and rugs. Zack and Uta rushed with Spider Grandma to take everything down. A moment later, the summer rain began to fall in drenching sheets, slapping the canvas roof, then rolling off onto the ground in a torrent.

THE MOUNTAIN

*U*ta couldn't forget her grandmother's vision of a death, the chilling dream that the old woman said had come to her on the wind. She hadn't forgotten it because Spider Grandma was never wrong about her visions. Once she had told a miner that she had a vision his Saint Bernard dog would die on that day.

"How?" the miner had asked. "I left my dog at home. He's in the house. There's no way he could die."

"I saw a necklace of blood," Spider Grandma had told him. "Your dog will wear a necklace of blood."

"You're crazy," the miner had said, and stormed off. That night when he got back to his cabin, he found the massive carcass of his dog hanging in the broken front window. The dog had tried to get out by jumping through the glass, but jagged pieces had ripped high into its throat. A cascade of scarlet had flooded down onto the sill and porch—a caked and frozen waterfall of blood. Spider Grandma had other visions, too, about ghosts causing illnesses where the only cure was dancing—and once she dreamed that the meat of a badger would cure a foot ailment. All had been true.

Uta called her mother and father and told them she and Zack would be sleeping over her grandmother's that night, then going on a camping trip for a few days.

"Won't they worry?" Zack asked Uta.

"No," Uta said. "They are never afraid for me in the wilderness. They taught me how to live and survive in it. All the Ute kids are raised that way. Growing up on my reservation is like one long survival course."

Spider Grandma set up cots for them all to sleep on in the main tent. She put down a plate of boiled duck hearts and feet for Picasso. Within minutes after she'd crawled into bed, she was snoring.

In the morning, the sun blazed down to dry the tent and sandy ground that surrounded the stand. By the time Zack and Uta had woken up and washed, Spider Grandma had taken a walk with Picasso and had coffee and fresh bread waiting for them.

"Will the cell phone work inside the mountain?" Uta asked.

"When you are near a main shaft," Spider Grandma said. She scribbled a number on a piece of paper and gave it to Zack. "This is the pay phone outside my tent. You call me every few hours. If I don't hear from you, I will know you are lost and send Larry Ghost Coyote and Uta's brothers to round you both up. Remember: follow only the cave drawings of the flute players and the climbing ropes!"

"Got it," Zack said.

Zack put Picasso into his little trailer and climbed onto the motorcycle. "Thank you, Spider Grandma," he said. Uta gave her grandmother a big hug and a kiss, then swung up behind him. He started the motor.

"I hope you find what you are looking for," Spider Grandma called as they drove off. "Picasso must miss this pet called Honker, too!"

Zack opened the throttle and raced the bike up toward the speed limit. Picasso began biting at the wind. "You don't have to come with me," Zack told Uta. "What if we meet one of the big ones again?"

"I'm going," Uta said, determined. "Just slow down before the wind tears my hair out."

By noon they had stopped at a convenience store. Uta

had money to fill up one of the saddlebags with sandwiches and bottles of apple juice, and they headed back to Zack's house. As they drove up, they noticed that the boards across the mangled front entrance were still in place. There were no signs any raptors had come back during the night.

Zack circled the house with the motorcycle, before parking in the breezeway. He let Picasso out of the trailer and headed for the storage shed by the corral.

"My dad bought spelunking equipment to explore the caves," Zack said.

"What's *spelunking?*" Uta asked.

"Cave exploring," Zack explained, flinging open the door. A pile of motley supplies were clustered at one end of a worktable. He picked out the gear he wanted, including ropes, flares, and a pair of spelunking helmets with double flashlights mounted on top of them.

"Check the batteries," Zack said, handing Uta the helmets. He crammed the rest of the equipment into one of the empty saddlebags.

"What about Picasso?" Uta asked.

"He's coming with us."

"Are you crazy?"

"I'm not leaving him."

"He'll end up as a dino snack!"

"No way. He handled himself fine with the mother raptor. He can run circles around any dinosaur. Besides, he's my pal!" Zack climbed onto the motorcycle and started the engine.

"Well, don't say I didn't warn you," Uta said, swinging up behind him. "I think he looks like a walking coconut ball." She held on to Zack's waist as he raced the bike down toward the highway.

"He'll be fine."

"What's the rush?" Uta asked.

"Bones'll be over snooping," Zack said. "He'll want brownie points for checking on me. He'll see that the door of the house was torn off. He's a paleontologist— he'll know what's going on."

Zack turned up the speed. He knew how Bones's mind worked, how greedy he was and what a power trip he was on. "We've got a few hours' head start before he'll follow us. He'll put my dad's accident together with the claw marks on the house. That'll lead him to the rockslide and Silver Mountain."

The afternoon sun blazed down on them as they neared the power dam and crossed over the crest road. Uta signaled to make a sharp turn down a dirt road that snaked steeply until it ran level with the spillway at the bottom.

"You know the entrance your grandmother marked on the map?" Zack asked.

"Yes," Uta said. "When I worked here I used to take tour groups down in the elevators. She wants us to go in through what used to be one of the commercial caves. A franchise owned it and used to sell tickets. It had lights and railings, but the tour only went into the mountain for a few hundred yards. The company that was running the cave went bankrupt, and the state closed everything except for self-tours of the dam. You can still see the turbines and generators, but there are no more guides. No more going down inside the caves."

The dirt road snaked along in the shadow of the looming dam. "That's where we go in," Uta said, pointing to a narrow stream that flowed out of the mountain and emptied into the spillway. Zack slowed the motorcycle and drove along a gravel path lining the stream. For a distance they were in a gorge, a cut in the mountain that grew sharper, narrower. The remnants of rusted railings and sand-covered footpaths built by the cave franchise surrounded them.

"A raptor could be around here, you know," Zack said.

"No," Uta said. "Too busy. There are lots of inspectors that drive around. Engineers. Men who fix the power lines. Raptors aren't stupid. They can't be if they've survived this long."

Zack thought the gorge looked like a carved, ancient temple. Layers of shale and petrified sediment rose high on the sides, time lines that marked the passing of millions of years. Soft rock had broken off in squares and rectangles, geometric erosions that gave an eerie, sculpted look. As the slit of sky narrowed, the slopes became encrusted with vines, enormous clusters of lilies, and half-rooted trees clinging desperately to promontories.

They passed the point where the gorge became a covered, darkening cave. The last rays of light struck thick layers of moss, which had blanketed the rocks. Leaves and logs that had floated into the cave were blackened with rot. Small, translucent trout moved in the pools of the stream. Cave crickets hopped everywhere.

"They have bugs in here," Uta said. "I had to learn a whole spiel for the tour, like how caves have some kinds of things that can live only part-time in a cave, and other stuff like eyeless fish, white crayfish, and blind beetles that can live their whole lives here. I never saw any of those."

The path curved and became part of the stream. The headlight caught the first of the stalactites hanging from the roof of the cave.

"This is as far as we go on the bike," Zack said. They

got off and put on their spelunking helmets. He let Picasso out of his trailer, and they split up the food and gear into their backpacks.

"That's where we go," said Zack, looking into a black hole from which the stream flowed.

He turned on the lights on their helmets and took off his sneakers. They rolled the bottom of their jeans up and started along the left side of the stream. "It's shallow," Zack said.

"It's narrow," Uta complained.

"Don't worry. I read once that passages of caves never stay narrow for very long."

Picasso drank from the cold running water. He wagged his tail and was confident when the water barely covered his feet. He began to dash around Zack in widening circles, until he was happily swimming out into the middle of the stream, then returning to the shallows.

Uta found the water chilling on her feet. "Hey, slow down," she yelled ahead.

"Come on," Zack called back.

It took Uta a while to get used to the light beams that shot out straight ahead from her helmet. As long as she looked straight at what she wanted to see, there was light, but to both sides of her was darkness. She heard Zack calling, "Honker! Honker!"

"You're nuts! You-know-who is going to hear you, too," Uta said.

"He might've gotten away from her."

"No way."

They trekked into a wider expanse. The stream was thirty to forty feet wide here, and flowed around mounds of massive white-and-yellow stalagmites. In the combined light from their helmets, they saw the limestone and dolomite drippings had taken fantastic shapes. There were points and cones and spirals like beautiful, glistening daggers protruding from everywhere. Uta's thoughts drifted back to Spider Grandma and her remembrance of other worlds.

Uta used to ask her grandmother about everything. About love and sex and death, and why they were born as Indians. She would stop by the stand every day with a new tale of some animal she'd found. Uta knew how to set a chipmunk's broken paw or feed a fallen eaglet from an eyedropper. She'd tell Spider Grandma about a mouse she'd saved from a well, or how she helped pick ticks off a fevered horse. She dreamed of becoming a veterinarian or a zoologist and her grandmother always encouraged her to follow those dreams.

Uta became aware of the stream bottom softening, her feet sinking deeper the farther they went.

"Did you check the map for quicksand?" she called to Zack.

Zack opened the plastic bag, took out the map, and looked at it. "No quicksand around here," he said.

Uta glanced down at the water for a moment. The reflection of the flashlights blinded her. When she looked up, Zack had disappeared around a bend. Her heart began to race. Keep calm, she told herself. Don't let Zack think you're a baby.

She moved forward, trying to concentrate on the area between herself and the bend. The water was up to her knees now. She plodded straight through the bottom mud. With each step, ooze slipped up through her toes.

She cried out as her right foot suddenly slid out from under her. Before she knew it she was sitting waist deep in the stream, her left foot doubled up beneath her.

Zack came rushing back around the bend with Picasso. "What's the matter?"

"My right foot's stuck!"

"The mud's thick here." He gripped her under her arms and tried lifting her up. He couldn't.

"Ahhh!"

"What?"

"Something's moving on top of my leg! Oh, my God, I can *feel* it."

Zack chuckled. "It's all in your mind. There's nothing. Probably just weeds. Weeds—"

"Stop laughing and get my leg out! It's in some kind of a *hole!*"

The helmet lights reflected off a long dark ribbon drifting toward them. Uta saw it and began screaming, "SNAKE! SNAKE!"

Zack waded forward and intercepted it. "It's a plain black snake, not a poisonous one," he said, tossing it away from Uta. "I thought you loved everything about the wilderness."

"I'm sorry. I don't like snakes!"

"Lean on me," Zack said.

Uta looked around, half expecting a raptor to jump from the shadows at any second. Zack traced with his hands down her right leg and into the mud in front of her. "It feels like there's a pole laying on top," he said. "Like your leg slipped under a rotting log."

"Pull it off!"

Zack slipped his hand around the log, grabbed it, and began to pull upward.

"It's coming," he said.

"Something's wiggling." Uta groaned. "The *log's wiggling!*"

Zack lifted the dark shape to the surface. "It looks like a . . ." He was about to say *stump*, when he realized the stump had slimy, moving barbs. A moment later, he was aware that the "log" had a huge, glistening black face and glaring yellow eyes. The form exploded into life, bursting free of the water and Zack's hands. Uta shrieked as the creature convulsed in the air, then splashed back down on top of her. Zack screamed with Uta. She struggled to stand up. Picasso barked as the squirming dark mass swam away downstream.

"What was it?" Uta shouted. *"What?"*

"A catfish!" Zack said, a shudder running through him. He started wiping off the slime from his hands on the wet gravel. "A giant catfish! We'd better find a place to get out of the water."

"Right!"

Zack put his arm around her to help her walk. "It's getting deeper, but here's a big chamber just around the bend."

Uta saw rays of sunlight pouring down from a gash in a dome. She broke away from Zack and was the first to scamper out of the stream and onto the floor of a massive cave chamber. "It's dry," she cried. "At least it's dry. Let me see the map."

Zack caught up to her and turned over the plastic bag. She took out the map. "Where are we?"

Zack pointed to a squiggly black line at the bottom of

the map. "This is the stream we just came out of," Zack said. "The one with the long Indian name."

"I see it, all right. And I know what the long Indian name translates to, too," Uta said.

"What?"

"*The Stream of Big Catfish.*" She rubbed at her jeans. "Turn around and don't look," she ordered, shivering.

Zack looked away as she slipped off her jeans and twisted them to wring out the water. "Good. At least I'm not soaking now, just wet," she said, putting the jeans back on. "Why is it hot down here?"

"The cave wind's blowing in from the south," Zack said. "There are cracks all over the ceiling."

"Then it's a good time to call Spider Grandma."

Zack took the cell phone out of his backpack and dialed the number Spider Grandma had scribbled onto a piece of paper. He handed the phone to Uta but moved close to the receiver so he could hear, too. There were several rings before someone answered.

"Hello," came Spider Grandma's voice.

"Grandma, it's me," Uta said.

"Is everything okay?"

"Yes."

"I'm glad you called," Spider Grandma said. "Something's come up with Dr. Bones."

"What?"

"Larry Ghost Coyote told me Bones is mounting a search team from a base camp at the Flaming Gorge dam."

"Bones must know about the raptors," Zack said.

"I'm not sure what he knows," Spider Grandma said. "I'm closing up to check it out. I borrowed another cell phone from the Kidney Lake diesel station. Only the last four digits are different: 7176. Like the date of the American Revolution, but mix it up a little. All I know is that Bones is buying up every shotgun, crossbow, and bazooka he can get his hands on!"

APPROACHING . . .

Picasso raced toward the center of the huge chamber. He began to sniff at the ground and stalk a scent in ever-widening circles. "We've got to hurry and find Honker," Zack said, "or Bones is going to have every local trapper hunting down here."

Uta followed Zack, weaving through a forest of yellow-and-red stalagmites.

"You know, I've been wondering why you don't like it here in Utah," Uta said. "Maybe you just weren't doing anything. What you needed was a raptor hunt where you might be eaten at any minute. That probably makes you feel like you're back in L.A. You know, drive-by devourings . . ."

Zack smiled, but his eyes searched carefully about the vastness of the great cave. He decided to take out one of the flares from his backpack and light it. The flare sparked, then began to glow with a steady light. Here, the cave and the mine blended into a mixture of man-made gizmos and startling nature. The far end of the cave narrowed as if it were a huge, glistening throat, stalactites hanging everywhere like icicles. The sides of the cave were lined with rows of ornate limestone towers. Elevated ore chutes and mine car railways shot every which way through the space like swords thrust into a huge magician's cabinet.

Uta checked the map. "There are supposed to be petroglyphs somewhere around here."

"There," Zack said, turning the lights from his helmet onto a tremendous slab of granite looming beside the entrance to a tunnel. The paintings at the center of the slab were hunting scenes, bowmen confronting a quarry of bighorn sheep. Below them were charcoal and pigmented drawings of snakes, and shamans in horned headdresses with rainbow-colored feathers. Closest to the tunnel entrance itself was a distinct rendering of a flute player with a rope dancing upward.

"The safe route must be the tunnel," Uta said.

Zack didn't answer. He was busy watching Picasso. The dog had stopped circling. "Why's he staring up at the ore chutes?" he said.

Uta turned to look. The lights on her helmet shot out across the expanse and lit up the chutes and mine tracks. She turned back to examine the petroglyph nearest the chutes. There were paintings of immense furry beasts with huge teeth and multiple heads. One monster was shown flying with a bleeding fox in its jaws. "Spider Grandma said that the monster drawings will only lead to death," Uta said. "We have to follow the flute player and dancing rope."

"Listen," Zack said.

"What?"

"Just *listen*."

Finally, Uta heard sounds—as though the highest reaches of the cave were whispering. "It's probably the wind."

"No," Zack said. "It's like . . . *growling*."

"We have to follow the flute—"

"I'll check out the chutes."

"No—"

"You wait here," Zack said.

"Call Spider Grandma back," Uta said. "Let's ask her." She grabbed the cell phone, pulled up its antenna, and held the receiver up to her ear. "There's no dial tone."

"We've moved deeper into the cave."

"Then let's go back."

The flare began to sputter and went out. Zack considered a retreat—but he remembered his father. How overworked and depressed he'd become under Bones's thumb. He knew his father was counting on him, believed he had made a great find—something that would change their lives forever.

He thought of Honker.

"I've got to check the chutes," Zack said, grabbing his gear. "Bones'll be all over this place by nightfall."

"Hey!" Uta shouted. "You're not leaving me here." She dashed after him as he strode up the main ramp. Picasso scooted ahead of both of them. "Spider Grandma said someone's going to die a horrible death," Uta reminded Zack.

"It was a vision. . . . A dream."

"Yeah, but her visions have a funny way of coming true."

Several of the rickety tracks and chutes crossed each other on a large wooden platform that jutted out from the cave wall. Uta checked the map as she walked to the edge of a drop-off that disappeared into a black pit. "The map calls this 'Devil's Slide.'"

"Where does it go?"

Uta turned her helmet lights so they shot down into the blackness. The rock was covered with a slippery moss, and the drop curved sharply out of sight like a laundry chute. "Not anyplace good," she said.

Picasso trotted to the mouth of the longest chute and started to whine.

"Is Honker this way?" Zack asked Picasso. "Is he, boy?"

Picasso's whine became a howl, and he started out onto the ramp. The flooring of the ramp was a badly worn conveyor belt. They followed Picasso. The chute led higher and higher above the floor of the cave. Uta stared over the sides and down the fifty foot drop to the bed of pointed stalagmites. She moaned.

"We've got to move it," Zack said, picking up the pace.

They continued down the longest stretch of the chute toward the center of the cave where another ramp fed in to join it. Uta held onto the wooden sides of the chute for balance. The cave was darker, and her hand brushed against something.

"Zack?"

"What?"

"I feel something—something *hairy* on the inside of this chute."

Zack let his hands swing out into the shadows of the railings. He could feel something strange, too. He stopped and knelt down. At first, he thought the sides were lined with a dark rug or blanket. The lights from his helmet made the insulation undulate—move.

Uta slowly knelt beside Zack and looked closer.

Closer.

They both froze, then screamed as the sides of the chute became a flutter of shiny membranes—thousands of little wings. The entire blanket came violently alive as a horde of bats rose about them, flying rodents with wet, hideous mouths and beady eyes. Uta screamed and the chute shook crazily. It seemed it would break loose from its moorings, drop, and shatter onto the limestone daggers below.

The massive cloud of bats washed over Uta and Zack. Uta thrashed, threw up her hands to protect her face and keep the bats out of her hair. Picasso snapped at the air and barked. The cloud of winged rats lifted, the fluttering mass zooming high toward dark places in the dome.

After a long while, Uta calmed. She checked her arms and face for scratches and bites. Zack could see she was close to tears. "A fine zoologist I'd make," she mumbled.

"At least it wasn't any kind of large critter," Zack said. "I mean, it wasn't wildcats or anything like that."

"Yeah, but I like normal wild animals in normal quantities. There's nothing normal about this place!" She used her hand as a comb, searching through her hair for any stray bats.

"There's nothing," Zack said.

Picasso whined again and moved forward on the ramp.

"He's onto something," Zack said.

Uta trailed Zack silently as they continued farther out on the ore chute. She kept looking straight ahead to a point where a second chute branched into the one they were on. She wondered what new horrors were waiting for them. "This ramp . . . this whole thing is vibrating," Uta said.

Zack felt the sway and movement.

"You're right."

They looked at each other.

"I don't feel so good," Uta said. "Like I'm going to engage in reverse peristalsis."

"Puke?"

"Yes."

"Maybe you should sit down a while?"

"No," Uta said. "There's probably guano all over with rabies and nits in it. I just want to get off this thing."

She stuck closer to Zack, her head spinning to check all around them. She could hear her lungs sucking air now, as Zack moved ahead step-by-step. She knew the loud thumping she could hear was her own blood pulsing through her temples. She began to worry that something large and hideous was about to come out of the darkness behind her, so she moved quickly in front of Zack.

Zack stared at something coming around the corner from the connecting ramp. "How cute," he said. "A puppy."

Uta looked up to see what he was talking about. Picasso had already frozen like a birddog pointing at the tiny intruder. At first the little animal seemed like a young collie or German shepherd. Then three massive stark white animals trotted out onto the ramp next to the pup. The flashlights reflected in their eyes, making them look like demons.

The animals shook their heads nervously, neurotically. They curled their snouts back. A series of growls slid out from between shining, saliva-drenched teeth.

Zack and Uta slowly—quietly—started to back up.

"What are they?" Zack asked.

Uta said, "Some kind of . . . WOOOOOOOOLVES!" She spun away from the snarling beasts. She knew they weren't normal wolves. Normal wolves don't attack humans. They were larger. Some kind of mutant trogloxenes, or cave visitors—animals that commonly enter caves but do not live in them.

Zack saw Uta and Picasso running back the way they'd come, and he started sprinting after them. The moment he moved, the wolves broke into a frenzy of howling. With teeth bared, they bolted forward after him.

Uta felt the chute sway sharply from the weight of the chase. She glanced over her shoulder. In the flickering light, she saw the largest wolf leaping into position as the front-runner. She and Zack shrieked. Picasso yelped.

Zack caught up to Uta quickly. "Faster!" he shouted. "Go faster!"

"I can't!"

"I'm going to run up your back!"

Several planks shook loose and dropped down to shatter on the stalagmites.

"AWWWWWWW, JEEZ," she heard Zack wailing.

Uta tripped as her foot tore through a section of the rotting conveyor belt. Zack yanked her upright, shoved her onward, back into a run. The wolves closed in on them, howling and snapping, hungrier now—as though they could taste the kill.

"Devil's Slide!" Zack yelled.

"What?"

"Jump into Devil's Slide!"

"ARE YOU CRAZY?"

"It's our only chance!"

Uta was the first to reach the main platform from which they had started. She scooped up Picasso and backed toward the wet black hole.

"GO! GO!" Zack shouted.

"NO!"

Zack hit the platform with the wolves snapping at his heels. "*DO* IT!"

Uta turned, still holding Picasso, and jumped. The lead wolf closed for a kill as Zack leaped after Uta into the dark hole. He felt the slime of half-rotting algae and moss, and heard Uta shrieking anew below him. Zack counted the seconds as he dropped, sliding over rock after rock—one, two, three seconds—finally he was free-falling toward Uta's screams and Picasso's frantic barking.

When he landed, the lights on his helmet lit up Uta flailing, struggling against a dozen open jaws—her arms and legs caught in tremendous slabs of teeth. He saw her hitting, kicking at the beasts, and he felt his own arms slipping into a pair of gaping jaws. He screamed along with Uta, again and again, as he waited for the pain and the blood and death.

Instead, Picasso ran over to him and started licking his face.

It took a few moments more before they realized that all of the teeth and jaws were parts of dead animals. Skulls and bones and claws of wolves and bears and raccoons.

"It's some kind of . . . graveyard," Zack said, gasping for breath. "A boneyard of dead . . . animals."

Uta stopped screaming. Reflexively, she gave the harmless bones and skulls several more kicks, and then burst into tears.

"I don't need *this* much wilderness," she sobbed. "This cave is crazy. There aren't any rules. Everything's a mutation!"

Picasso scooted to her and started licking one of her ears. Zack straightened his helmet, crawled across the bed of bones to her, and put his arm around her. "Hey, come on, now. Everything's fine. We're safe."

"And the wolves?"

He pointed. "Up there—I hope."

Zack took a tissue from his jeans and wiped at the tears on her face. "What is this horrible place?" Zack asked.

She looked around and saw how huge a pile of bones they'd landed on. "I think it's where something dumps its leftovers." She noticed half the skulls were cracked and most of the bones were shattered. "Something kills animals, eats their flesh, then dumps the bones here when it's finished. Terrible housekeeper. And I can imagine who."

"Oh, God," Zack said.

"What?"

"I'm hungry and I don't feel like eating a sandwich or a grub. I wish we were in an L.A. mall," he said. "We could get a slice of pizza, or share a chocolate chip cookie—or go see a movie . . ."

Uta put her finger up to his mouth. "Shhhh."

"What?"

"Honking," Uta said, staring down into a long, dark tunnel. "I hear *honking.*"

Dr. Boneid coughed in the gray dust of the dam's parking lot as he got out and slammed the Rover's door. He shook hands with Manny Spencer and Eric Gonzales, the only workers and drinking buddies he trusted on the dig. He had told them what they were really stalking, and they had already organized the lot into something resembling a small army base.

"You find Professor Norak's rockslide?" Boneid asked. "Where he had his stupid accident?"

"Yep," Eric said. "It's a mine entrance higher on the north slope." He pointed to a map. "Right here."

"He was as dumb as a box of rocks messing around up there," Manny said in his South Carolina accent. "We found what was his mule. More guts than you can shake a stick at—something tore its head off."

Boneid thought that over a moment. "That's too bad,"

he said. His eyes searched the parking lot. He was glad to see they'd brought his air-conditioned trailer up from the dig. "Did the Kinski brothers get down here with their bear traps?"

"Yeah," Manny said. He was a barrel-chested stub of a man, in his mid-forties and the best rifle shot in eastern Utah.

"They've got another trapper on his way from Meeks Cabin Reservoir," Eric said. "He's got a tranquilizing gun that'll put a grizzly to sleep at a hundred yards." Eric was younger, taller, and more muscular. He had a shock of dirty-blond hair over intense, crazy eyes.

"It'd better be able to take down an elephant," Boneid said, spitting on what was left of the Rover's corroded hood. "We're going to need it."

Spencer and Gonzales fell in step next to Dr. Boneid as he set off to check the equipment. A dozen or so rusting trucks and vans with mirror ornaments, rifle racks, and crude bumper stickers were parked by the dam's maintenance shed. Boneid had pulled in every chip he had with the parks commissioner and Flaming Gorge Dam authorities. He'd told everyone that he'd spotted a large lizard and that he wanted to trap it. No big deal.

Nothing much.

He didn't tell anyone except Manny and Eric that he

was after a living dinosaur! No one had to know he was euphoric with the possibilities of what capturing one would mean. The celebrity. The money. The merchandising. It was a paleontologist's ultimate trip. He was sure they'd catch the young raptor, but they'd probably have to blow the head off the big one to get it.

"You've got the blueprints on the mine?" Boneid asked.

"In your trailer," Manny said. "The parks commissioner sent them right over, along with one of his top engineers in the water control offices. He says if you need water, he'll give you all you want faster than a house afire."

Boneid smiled. It always amazed him how far a couple of lunches and gift bottles of champagne went with the local movers and shakers.

"Dr. Bones!" one of the workers called out from the shade of a tent.

"Hey there," Boneid called back, mumbling, pretending he remembered his name. He waved to a handful of Mexican workers setting out carbide lamps, flashlights, and other spelunking equipment. He liked it when anyone called him "Dr. Bones." He'd created the name for the media. He thought it would be catchy. Folksy. Help propel him to fame and glory. No point in sounding like some two-bit stuffy scholar.

"You bring up the dumdum shells and dynamite from the dig?" Boneid asked.

"Yeah," Manny said. "We got bullet tips that'll rip the heart out of Godzilla. Plenty of double-loaded ammo for the shotguns, not as strong—but better than a poke in the eye with a burned stick."

Boneid halted by a long, air-conditioned horse trailer. Workers lowered a ramp from the back of the trailer like it was part of an overnight circus. There was a rumbling as the Kinski brothers supervised rolling down a six-foot metal cage with glimmering two-inch bars of steel.

"Nice cage, eh?" Eric said.

"Yeah," Boneid agreed. "For the little one."

He stopped and looked up to the north slope of the mountain. "Did you clear the slide yet?"

Eric scratched at the two-day stubble on his chin. "Yeah."

"Then let's get the lead out," Dr. Boneid said. "A little recon before the main search." He saw his hands were beginning to shake. "I'll follow you on up."

DARK SANCTUM

*D*evil's Slide was much too slippery for Zack and Uta to climb back up. The only escape from the pit of bones was down, deeper through a cave passage with a mist that was so thick it tasted of death. The passage grew narrower, and a wind began to roar into their faces. Uta tied her hair back from her face and Picasso bit at the air.

"Be alive, Honker," Zack muttered, half to himself.

"Those sounds might be another baby raptor—not Honker," Uta said. "And even if we find him, how are we going to get him away from his mother?"

Zack shook his head and admitted, "I don't know."

The sounds were more distant now—as though Honker was being taken farther into the very center of the mountain—but there were other sounds as well. Shrieks and roars like they'd heard from the mother raptor. Gurgling sounds of underwater streams. And low-pitched cries like lions fighting over carrion in a jungle.

Manny strapped on his rifle and climbing gear as Eric drove their Jeep up the rough road to the rockslide. They laughed about Dr. Boneid, following behind them in the Rover.

"Bonehead!" Eric said. "Seeing living dinos! What a laugh!"

"He must have been stewed!" Manny laughed. All Eric had to do was mention the word *dinosaur* or *raptor*, and Manny howled.

"Yeah, boys," Eric said, imitating Boneid's raspy voice, "today we're going on a raptor hunt!"

"Stop it!" Manny yelled, clutching his sides. "It hurts. Hurts!"

"Yes, men—see, this dino came out of the fog and jumped me faster than a duck on a June bug. And when the big dino opened its mouth, guess what was inside?"

Manny screamed with laughter. "A little dino!"

"Right!"

The way Manny and Eric saw it, Bones had had a few drinks too many and come across a grizzly and her cub. All he'd probably seen was some big shadows and waving claws, and all he'd heard was a couple of roars. A spooked grizzly was hard enough to catch without making believe it was some kind of a cockamamy dino.

Another thousand feet higher on the mountain there was a break in the evergreens and they could see the craggy peaks and badlands east of the dam. Roots of massive pines had gouged their way into the sandstone cliffs. The wound of the rockslide lay dead ahead.

They parked at the end of the rutted road, unloaded their equipment, and carried it up the slope to the rockslide and mine entrance.

"I don't want you going in deep," Boneid said, puffing as he caught up. "Stay in touch with your walkie-talkie. Just get an idea of what we're getting into."

"Right, boss," Eric said, giving Manny a wink. He and Manny turned on their flashlights and started off with their rifles ready. Boneid checked his pistol in its holster to make certain it was loaded, and sat in the shadows of the entrance. He let them get a ways inside before he tested his walkie-talkie. "Hello," he said.

"We hear you," Manny's voice came from the receiver.

"Good." Boneid watched the silhouettes of the two men growing smaller as they moved a distance into the mine. He knew they were both experienced spelunkers. If there was anything to be found in the high tunnel, they'd find it. *Shoot the big one. Catch the little one.* He'd made that clear to them.

"Something big came through here," Eric said. They stepped on broken pieces of stalagmite and stalactites, which lay strewn on the floor.

"Yeah," Manny said. He kept his flashlight trained on the floor. He was the first to smell the bad odor and see more chunks of the mule's carcass splattered at the base of a wall. Beyond, he saw a circle of vegetation in a dark cranny of the tunnel. He and Eric checked the vomit-covered leaves and small, shredded leathery sacks that were crawling with maggots.

"We've found something that looks like . . . like where some animal sleeps, Dr. Bones," Eric said, into the walkie-talkie. "Like a nest. It's got weird ripped packets in it with worms crawling all over them."

"Could they be pieces of shells? Some kind of eggs?" Dr. Bones said, his voice crackling with excitement.

"Could be," Manny said.

Manny and Eric fought to stifle their laughter. They'd seen bears make all kind of nests in caves and stash lots of stuff in them, just like rats and mice do. It looked like this bear had found some kind of a tire tube and bitten it to pieces.

"How many shells?" Dr. Boneid asked.

Eric counted. "About a dozen, maybe."

"Bring me one out—now!" Dr. Boneid's voice came over the walkie-talkie. "I want to see it before you go any farther."

Eric pointed to Manny.

Manny scowled. "You wait till I come back, okay?" he whispered.

"Yeah."

Manny returned to the nest, took a small collapsible shovel from his backpack, and scooped up one of the torn leather packets—worms and all. He started back toward the tunnel exit.

Eric waited for a few moments. He began to feel cold standing in one spot.

SCRATCH. SCRAAAATCH

He heard the sounds coming from just ahead—around a bend in the tunnel. He shifted his rifle, released its safety, and started forward. The sounds weren't from a large animal. It couldn't be much more than cave squirrels or a young cougar. Maybe the grizzly cub, he thought. For a moment he had a fantasy about catching a bear cub, just picking it up and bringing it out for Bones to see. He'd probably get a bonus, or they'd let him sell it. He knew one of the Utes who had gotten five thousand dollars from a St. Louis zoo for a baby grizzly.

He looked down, saw a wide scraping trail, as though someone had dragged a sack along the dirt floor. There were tracks in the dust, small, most of them four-toed. Three thick toes and a fourth smaller one.

He let his flashlight cut into the darkness of the bend. A few steps further on, he saw a wet spot, a small dark pool that had spilled and caked on the ground.

SCRATCH.

Suddenly, a lizard appeared from one of the alcoves along the wall. It was the largest lizard he'd ever seen, bigger and thicker than any iguana or anything down in Mexico. He had always liked iguanas. He had photos from home of lizards coming up to him and taking hibiscus flowers from between his teeth.

"Hey, guy," Eric said.

Maybe Bones had seen a lizard, he thought. He was probably in one of his stupors and just thought it was big. He could imagine what Bones would do if he came out of the tunnel carrying it. And if it were a new kind of lizard, he knew Bones would take good care of him. A nice, juicy bonus. At least a couple of weeks off to go down and see his kids outside Mazatlán.

The lizard looked up at Eric. It stood up on its thick hind legs and cocked its head. It almost looked cute.

"Come here, guy," Eric said gently. He reached out

his hand, and moved forward slowly to pet it. "Come on. I won't hurt you." The lizard backed off, so he reached into his backpack, tore off a piece of a sandwich, and held it out.

At the sight of the food, the lizard stepped forward carefully, like a wild turkey pecking the ground for seeds. It came to within a foot of Eric's hand. Its eyes darted from the shred of a sandwich to the glint of the rifle barrel.

"The gun scaring you?" Eric asked. He set his rifle down next to the flashlight. "See, I'm not going to hurt you."

The lizard came closer now. It began to peck at the ham and cheese and bread. Eric kneeled. Slowly, he inched his left hand around the side of the lizard. It seemed tame, he thought. He knew there was a chance it could have been someone's pet, some weird tourist or gem hunter who'd let his pet lizard get away from him. More likely, he knew, was that the mountain—with all its abandoned mine shafts and caves—had protected its wildlife so much that it wasn't very wild anymore. He thought it might be like the Galápagos Islands, where the birds and lizards know no fear of man. He could see what a find it could be: Eric Gonzales, carrying the lizard out, letting Bonehead spin the mountain all over the world as the new Galápagos.

That would mean a lot of money for everyone, Eric knew.

Especially *him*.

SCRAAAAAATCH.

There were more sounds now. Suddenly, three more lizards emerged from the shadows and came right up to him. Then several more.

"Hi, guys," he said. He began to think about the lizards and the nest he'd seen. Lizards were reptiles, and reptiles had nests and eggs. He and Manny had only seen one nest, but that didn't mean there couldn't be others. Other nests and . . .

He realized he might have crawled too far from his rifle and flashlight. He smiled at the lizards and slowly began to inch back.

Two of the lizards leaped up onto his backpack. They felt twenty or thirty pounds each.

Heavy.

"Hey, guys . . . ," he said.

The lizards pecked at the open zipper and grabbed the edges of the backpack. Soon, they had ripped the pocket open and tore into the rest of the sandwich. "That's not nice," Eric said, trying to keep his voice friendly. He knew wild animals could smell human fear. He was not afraid, he told himself.

There was no fear. He would just reach out to his rifle and . . .

He moved his hand slowly behind him, letting his fingers crawl to the gun. Another lizard rushed from the darkness and pecked violently at his hand like it was chicken feed.

"Ow," Eric yelled. He yanked his hand back and stared at the wound in the center of his palm. Blood was gushing out of it. "All right, playtime is over!" He swung his arms left and right, smacking a bunch of the lizards away. As he spun, he threw himself backward toward the rifle, but the horde of lizards shrieked and rebounded at him. Their beaklike jaws opened to reveal the sharp, pointed teeth that lined their mouths.

A couple of the lizards raced toward his legs and began to tear at them. Eric cried out. He would get the gun now and blow their heads off. He'd shoot them in the face, wallpaper the cave with their brains. He grabbed for the stock of the rifle, but a single lizard rushed forward and yanked it away.

He punched at the lizards now.

A dozen of them leaped up onto his neck and head.

He reached up to tear them off, but several others raced at his face. He felt their snouts biting, pecking, deep into his cheeks and eyes. Soon, he felt the warm flush of his blood pouring down his face, and blindness came quickly—painfully.

At the mouth of the tunnel, all Dr. Boneid and Manny could hear on the receiver was Eric Gonzales's screams. By the time they made it back inside the cave to where Manny had left him, Eric had disappeared. At the tunnel's bend were a few pools of blood and scuff marks in the dust.

Zack had lost track of how long they had been following the honking sounds, but he had to continue looking for Honker. He couldn't leave the mountain until he had the baby dinosaur back. No matter what, he would bring Honker out. For his father. For the sake of the whole Norak family.

For Honker.

Deeper inside the cave, the wind howled eerily as if somewhere a single, deep note was being played on a cello. The passageway curved and they saw a glint of light ahead. A series of mine shafts rose from the cave ceiling— straight up for over a thousand feet to the slopes of the mountain. Water trickled across the floor in small, crooked grooves. The light from Zack's flashlight bounced off ghostly swellings that hung on the cave walls.

"What are those?" Uta wanted to know.

"They look like . . ." Zack went silent as he reached out and touched one of the strange white sacks. Something long and black twitched under the mesh and webbing. "It looks like there's a fish inside," Zack said. "One of the big catfish—in something like a cocoon."

He looked closer, then corrected himself. "Half a catfish."

"What do you mean, *half* a catfish?"

"Its tail . . . and chunks of its body . . . are missing."

"Oh, my . . ." Uta shivered. She looked away from the strange, dripping sack. A short distance farther, the sacks were larger, more plentiful. Within a hundred feet, they were hanging in clusters—nearly blocking the passageway, like the carcasses in a butcher's freezer.

Zack shone the light from his helmet onto one of the larger shapes. He gasped when he found himself staring into the veiled face of a beast. "What is that?"

Uta moved closer, peered through the weblike mesh. "I think it's a bear," she said. "Part of a bear. It's missing its . . . legs."

"What happened to them?"

"I can't see exactly . . . they look like they've been bitten or ripped off."

Uta gasped.

Zack made out a slow rising and falling of the creature's chest. "It's still breathing," he said. Picasso sniffed, and let out a mournful howl. Zack picked him up and petted him. "Shhhhh," he said.

"We'd better go back," Uta said.

Sounds.

Sounds behind them.

Zack moved quickly ahead through the maze of hanging pouches. Finally, the clusters gave way to a clearing with a towering wall of sacks. It looked like a huge honeycomb—fifty or sixty feet high—as if cave bees had created a stack of outsized storage cells. The lighted shaft behind the stack silhouetted the contents of the sacks: fish and eels, wolves and bears and wild horses. Some were whole animals. Most were mutilated. Pieces of the animals protruded through the sack membranes, heads and legs and tails bursting out like some sort of living, undulating collage. The gruesome wall made Zack halt in astonishment. "Is this what I think it is?"

"Yes, I think so," Uta said. "It's a *larder*. It's got to be where the raptors store their food."

"I don't understand."

"They must eat these things," Uta said, "but not all at once. Maybe it's some kind of rationing system—keep everything alive as long as possible, and then eat it one piece at a time. Like spiders do."

"That's horrible."

"Yes, but it's probably how they've managed to survive," Uta said.

"They could be brainy in really weird ways. My dad always thought raptors were the smartest of all the dinosaurs anyway."

Putrid juices, yellow and crimson, oozed from the sacks. Zack felt his stomach twist and roll. He looked away. The wind shifted and he began to choke. "Where are the raptors?" he asked anxiously. "Where are they?"

"The stench of the larder must be cloaking our scent," Uta whispered. "They would have found us long ago. Let's go . . ."

Zack slipped his hand over her mouth. "They're coming," he whispered.

He put out the lights on their helmets and gripped Picasso around his muzzle ready to squeeze tight if he tried to bark. It took a moment for their eyes to get used to the near darkness. There was movement in the shadows and side chambers ahead. Sounds came from the mouth of a dark tunnel at the base of the food wall.

Uta followed Zack into the maze of sacks. The sacks shifted and turned as they brushed against them. Uta groaned when she felt the oily, sticky fluids dripping on her.

The sounds were louder, closer now. Zack moved on until he found a good spot for them to hide behind a cluster of the hanging sacks.

ROAR.

The first of the adult raptors raced out from a shadowy side chamber into a clearing below the wall of prey. A half dozen other large raptors ran through a thick mist rising from the floor of the cave. They turned erratically, crying wildly at the wall. Zack saw Picasso's eyes grow as big as saucers, and he tightened his grip on the dog's snout.

There was another roar.

Louder.

Earsplitting.

Zack and Uta froze at the sight of a gargantuan creature materializing from the darkness. They gasped when they realized it was twice the size of Honker's mother, a bloated freak of a dinosaur barely recognizable as a raptor. Its back was completely black, with the caudal vertebrae of its tail gnarled and as thick as kegs. Its grasping forelimbs were swollen with muscle, and it had claws twice the size of the other raptors.

"Look at its jaws," Uta whispered. Fangs curved out over thick strips of cartilage. Several of them were so long and curled they circled and were beginning to pierce the creature's pebbled scalp.

"What is that thing?" Uta asked.

"God's sick joke," Zack said. A perfectly evolved killing machine. A monster beyond *T. rex*. Beyond *Gigantosaurus*. Something evolved further than any carnivore that had ever lived. The creature was absurd, but terrible and deadly—all rolled into one! The sight of the dinosaur made Zack's heart pound like a jackhammer. "It's the only one with a totally black back. It's a freak . . . a male . . . ," he said.

"How do you know it's a male?"

"Trust me."

"Oh."

The other raptors began to nudge several of the larger sacks and shriek at the giant raptor.

Zack stood on his toes to see over the cluster of sacks. "It's like Blackback is the protector of the larder. I think no one eats without checking with him. He's probably the big cheese at every kill."

Shrieking erupted from one side of the clearing. Three of the most fierce-looking raptors herded a fourth until it was delivered to face the giant raptor. Uta recognized the cuts and scrapes on its body. "That's Honker's mother," she whispered.

"Then maybe Honker's around," Zack whispered back.

The protector of the larder sniffed at Honker's mother. Other raptors made elaborate hissing and hacking sounds, and swung their tails.

Honker's mother was cowed into silence along with the rest of the group. The giant raptor brought its loathsome face closer to her snout. Slabs of animal skull and shreds of dried flesh were permanently impaled on several of the blackback's longer, swirling fangs. It seemed to be checking her mouth and groin and wounds for clues—where she had been and what she'd been doing.

He was interrupted by a burst of screeching, shrill sounds from a pack of juveniles as they dragged something out of the darkness and presented it to the blackback like an offering.

"What is it?" Uta asked. "I can't see."

Zack pushed against the cluster of sacks to shift them and raised himself up on tiptoe. "My God! It's Gonzales!" he said, shaking his head. "Eric Gonzales! Bones's foreman from the dig. They killed him! That means Bones and his crew have already started a sweep into the mountain."

"Maybe the raptors got all of them."

"I don't think so. . . ."

"What are they going to do to him?"

Zack watched horrified as, suddenly, the blackback sunk its giant claws deep into Gonzales's underbelly. It yanked its claws forward again and again, until the body yielded shreds, then whole chunks of flesh. The impact tumbled the body across the ground. The blackback chased it, pounced on it, and tore into Gonzales's left arm. It began devouring it right on his body. Within moments, there was a sickening ripping sound as the arm was stripped of muscle and sinew, leaving only gristle and bones.

Uta shifted so she could see what was going on out in the clearing. At the sight of the mutilation, a scream started up from her throat, but she cut it off. She began to hyperventilate, her heart pounding in her chest. She buried her head into Zack's shoulder, fighting to get her breathing back under control.

The other raptors frantically circled the blackback as he feasted on Gonzales's bleeding, shredded right arm. They began a high-pitched screeching, sounds that reverberated in the cave like chanting from a madhouse.

"They're waiting," Uta said.

"For what?"

"Their turn."

The blackback finally stopped eating. It backed away

from what was left of Gonzales's torso, threw its head back—and emitted a long, wavering shriek. The other raptors rushed forward to the carcass, ripping away big slabs of flesh with their teeth. With snouts dripping blood, juveniles dashed in and out of the frenzy, taking nips of his organs. Some of the young raptors ran off proudly dragging the wet, scarlet ribbons of his intestines.

With another roar, the blackback swung back to the carcass. The other raptors had seized a good share of the body and had raced away to finish their feasting in privacy. Gonzales's legs still twitched reflexively. The blackback hovered over him again and began to make new sounds, guttural ones from deep inside his body. Fluids sprayed from the blackback's mouth. He let the drippings fall over the gaping raw and red holes in Gonzales's body, making the wounds begin to steam and sizzle like frying bacon.

The smell of burning flesh filled the air.

Zack struggled to find words. "He's . . . cauterizing what's left of the body," he said. "He's *sealing* him."

The blackback sank its jaws into the nape of its victim's neck and swung the remains of his body up against a row of the sticky, hanging sacks. Other raptors ran forward and began to spray the carcass with other, whiter fluids. They helped spin the body, turn it, until the sprayed fluids from their mouths stiffened into fibers.

Zack gasped. "They've evolved . . . fluids. All kinds of . . . fluids . . ."

Uta had turned away. When she looked back at the wall of prey, she saw the remains of Gonzales hanging up in its own grisly white sack. His face had been half eaten by the baby raptors, dark, bleeding cavities where there had once been eyes. Zack, too, turned away. His instinct was to shield Uta, to put his arm around her, and move them both slowly back away from the larder. The abominable sight throbbed in his mind, and his knees had grown weak. Both he and Uta were choked with shock as they moved carefully away through the hanging sacks. They passed under one of the mine shafts. For a moment there was a circle of light and a breath of fresh air.

Then they heard a sound.

RING! RINNNNNNG!

The noise of a loud bell ringing. Ringing near them. A sound resonating in the cave.

"The phone!" Uta cried out. She grabbed it, and shut the ringer off, but it was too late. Every raptor in the clearing had turned to stare in their direction.

"Take Picasso and get out of here!" Zack ordered, pushing the dog into her arms.

"What about you?"

"Get help!"

"But . . ."

"NOW!"

Picasso barked as Zack turned back toward the raptors in the clearing. "I'M HERE! HERE I AM!" he began shouting at the top of his lungs. He headed straight toward the raptors.

Uta trembled in panic. It took her a moment to realize Zack was deliberately drawing the raptors away. "No!" she called hoarsely to him. "No!" She started after him, to make him turn and flee with her out of this unreal larder. "Zack!" she cried. He was sacrificing himself for her. She wanted to scream, as though that would make the nightmare go away, but she knew she wasn't dreaming. She understood that Zack's only chance—and her only chance—would be if she got out and brought back help.

Holding Picasso in her arms, she gripped his snout to quiet him as she sprinted through the maze of hanging white sacks. Paws, claws, pieces of animals hung out from the mesh, scratching her and catching on her clothes. She heard scurrying sounds, saw that there were hatchling-size raptors on her trail. They were scrawnier than Honker, but were still mean-looking eating machines. Several jumped out in front of her and she managed to kick one a good twenty feet.

The hatchlings snapped at her ankles as she ran. Picasso stared down at them and shook his snout loose of Uta's grasp. He barked at them, launched himself out of Uta's arms, and hit the ground running straight at them. He chased the chicken-size raptors away from Uta, growling at them fiercely.

"Picasso!" Uta called, as she fled. Picasso, like a border collie herding sheep, kept the little raptors scurrying away. They retreated through a maze of stalagmites. Picasso pursued them, confidently, ferociously. Suddenly, he raced around the base of a large stalagmite and found himself facing a couple of dozen of the nasty hatchlings. They were blocking his way.

Picasso stopped abruptly. For a moment, it seemed as if he was thinking things over. Suddenly, he let out a whine, whirled, and fled. The flock followed, shrieking, hungry for another kill.

SACRIFICE

Zack continued to shout as he broke loose from the cover of larder sacks. "LOOK HERE! HERE I AM!" For a moment he thought he would be attacked and killed instantly, but the raptors remained frozen—startled at the strange sight charging at them. "THAT'S RIGHT! LOOK AT ME! ONLY ME!" It was when he was certain that he'd completely drawn their attention, that an idea to save his own life clicked in.

The blackback was the first to register fury at the invasion. It rose up high on its haunches and shifted nervously. It began to hiss, flick its tongue over its crooked teeth, and finally opened its mouth into a roar. Zack noticed another tunnel and he began to think of an impossible, crazy escape for himself.

A delusion.

A dream.

"YEAH! LOOK AT ME! JUST LOOK AT ME!" he shouted and whistled. He made every nonsense sound and karate grunt he could think of, anything to keep the raptors paralyzed with surprise. In his fantasy born of fear, he would find Honker in the narrow tunnel. He'd find the baby dinosaur, without his vicious mother, and he and Zack would race down the tunnel. The other raptors would be amazed, even kind. They would understand that he meant no harm, and he and Honker would break out of the mountain and into the light of day. . . .

Zack didn't get ten feet past the raptors before the entire pack shrieked with rage. He kept his eyes glued on the entrance to the tunnel, as if his sanity depended upon believing he would escape. He heard motion, a raucous racing of bodies closing in on him. Out of the corner of his eye, he knew there were large creatures pursuing, attacking with the motion of ostriches.

"LET ME GO! JUST LET ME GO!" he shouted, when a blast of roars and shrieking exploded at his back. The first of the larger raptors thrust its jaws forward and bit into his neck. He felt himself being picked up, air-borne, and thrown backward like a rag doll. When he stopped rolling, blood was trickling down his back.

Zack staggered to his feet, with a ring of shrieking raptors around him.

ROAR.

ROARRRRRRR!

The ground shook as the blackback leaped to tower over him. Zack looked up—up!—into the massive, gnarled face. Just a bad dream, he began to tell himself. A very, very bad dream! Then the saliva with the stench of death spilled out from between the tusk-sized teeth to drip on Zack. His muscles stiffened as the blackback's forearms embraced him like a vise. He was lifted off the ground, held high in front of the glistening, gaping snout. A wet slime leaked from the blackback's nostrils, and its bulbous yellow eyes stared into Zack's soul.

Zack couldn't speak as he stared up into the monstrous face. Its stinking breath wheezed out through a green pus that trickled from the base of its rotting teeth. Closer, he found the smell that spilled from its lungs was beyond that of the fetid shreds of flesh and fresh bone that clung to its jaws. It smelled of tombs and sweat and worm-infested meat.

Slowly, the blackback stroked Zack's face with a claw. Its needle-thin, pointed tip touched Zack's forehead and then was drawn slowly down the left side of his face.

Between his screams, Zack thought of his father as the claw found the softness of his under chin.

EEEEEEEHHHHH!

Zack's body contorted, his high-pitched shrieking filling the air, as he felt the claw rising up through his chin. Why are you doing this? Zack wondered. Why did you do it to my father? He felt the finger of the claw pulsate, as if it were some sort of a tube. There was a hotness as a fluid was being released into Zack. A poison? Zack wondered. What? What would the fluid do? What did it mean? Am I dead?

Finally, the blackback pulled the claw tip out. Zack felt the release of the pressure, but he heard new sounds coming from the raptor's throat. There was a gurgling, and a gentle coughing. He was aware of losing consciousness. More than anything, he felt loss. The poison traveled quickly into his brain, and he understood his life was over. His dream of going back to L.A. seemed silly now. Foolish. Dreams of Malibu cars and Sunset Boulevard and Galleria friends.

He thought of Uta.

And Picasso.

His last conscious thought was of his father, and he felt a sadness deeper than death.

The raptor brought its mouth closer to Zack, as

though it were going to chew his face off. Instead, what looked like a large glob of spit rolled to the edge of the stinking mouth. With a final ritual, the blackback began to cover Zack with the spittle, letting it drip down over his eyes and neck and chest.

Uta heard Zack's scream as she raced up a rise at the end of the larder cave. She turned and looked across the vast, ghostly chamber. In the distant shadows—beyond the clusters of stalactites and gory sacks—she glimpsed Zack clutched by the monstrous raptor. She saw his body kicking and flailing like a marionette.

Help.

She would get help. It was the only thing her mind could accept, the only way she could keep running away. She saw a slab of eroded petroglyphs on a wall by an air shaft. Whole pieces of the stone were cracked and had fallen away. Parts had been vandalized long ago by miners, but there were the remnants of a flute player and a rising rope bordering a tunnel.

"Picasso!" she screamed a last time. If he heard her, he could catch up. If the young raptors had gotten him, she . . .

Uta realized she couldn't even think about it as she raced into the tunnel. She found herself praying, thinking of Spider Grandma and needing to believe that the flute player and rope meant she was going to escape the mountain. The tunnel was dark, and she stumbled on planking and chunks of granite and sandstone. She hit hard into the brittle stumps of stalagmites and flicked on the lights on her helmet.

The tunnel was straight, and finally there were nothing chasing her now but the echoes of her own footfalls. The beams of light reflected back from clusters of quartz and hematite in the walls. But there was a brighter light. Round and colorful and far off—as far as the distance she and Zack had traveled into the mountain. She could hardly run as her body trembled, and the truth began to take hold of her. She had heard Zack's screams. She had seen him gripped by the horrendous claws of the blackback.

Zack was dead.

She knew he was dead.

For a dinosaur, a baby dinosaur that probably didn't care that he existed.

Dr. Boneid left the dam's control turret with a smile on his face. He'd wanted to go over the plan with the engineers, to make certain nothing could go wrong. "I want the mountain flooded," Boneid had said. The Flaming

Gorge chief engineer explained that it wasn't a problem. There had been a contingency sluice built in place when the Gorge Recreation Area had first been conceived.

"The Magic Dog Canyon shunt of the reservoir hasn't been used in forty years," the engineer said. "It's been abandoned and all the hydraulics are rusted shut. Jammed. My inspector up there says the gates won't respond manually, but the commissioner says you can blow it if you have to."

"Good," Boneid said. "We have to."

"It'll put half the mountain underwater, you know."

"That'll be fine. How long will it take for the flood to hit down here?"

"We're talking several million cubic feet of water, through mainly narrow tunnels and constricted underground passages. About five or ten minutes after you blow the shunt."

Boneid had borrowed helicopters from two commercial pilots that hired out to hunters and tourists for flights into the back lakes and the gorge. He'd sent the explosives team from the university dig north to the Magic Dog Canyon shunt. They had already set massive charges, wired the detonators to timers, and were waiting for a "go" command.

A drenching sheet of fog crawled off the reservoir and

began to blanket the six-wheelers and vans in the parking lot. Tents had been rigged over portable generators that roared and shook the ground with spasms. Grids of floodlights blazed against the drifting wall of mist. Manny ran across a maze of power cables toward Boneid.

"I got eel traps in on the downstream," Manny said. "They'll scoop up a bat's ear if it floats out of that mountain. Seven riflemen who could shoot the whisper out of a whirlwind are on the upper shafts."

"All I need is proof of those dinos, I don't care if they're in pieces," Boneid said. "You tell the sharpshooters to be careful?"

Manny took a moment to catch his breath. "I told them they've got to shoot straight on this one or they'll end up being dined on like cat food. They don't like the idea of you flooding the mountain at all. There's a bunch of rain dancers running around the town trying to get a sheriff up here to stop you."

"What's their problem?"

"Some whining about all the wildlife that'll be destroyed. They think animals are people."

"Yeah. And they think God lives on the sun. What else is new?"

"Engineers confirm yet that only two tunnels would be left above the flood line?"

"Yes." Boneid felt sweat drop from his armpit. He went into his trailer. The radio transmitter in the office started beeping. He motioned Manny to answer it.

"It's Joey up at Magic Dog Canyon," Manny told Boneid. "They want to know if they've got a green light to blow it?"

Boneid took a moment to think. To daydream. He realized the significance of what was about to happen. Every natural history museum and society in the country—no, in the world!—would be waving money at him. Join our board, Dr. Boneid. Oh, please let us fund your next dig. Yes, let your fame and light and paleontological wisdom shine down on us!

There was a pounding on the trailer door.

"Who's that?" Boneid mumbled. He found a single wine glass and a jelly jar, and began to rinse them out, as Manny opened the door. There was one of the Ute men and some strange-looking old woman. He recognized Larry Ghost Coyote as one of the Utes that rented horses to the dig. The old lady wore bear-claw earrings and an embroidered black velvet shawl.

"Dr. Bones," she shouted as she pushed her way into the trailer. "You can't flood the mountain! There are two kids down there! Two kids!"

Uta broke out from the mountain on a slope near the bottom of a gorge. She was shocked to recognize the remnants of pipe railings and leveled footpaths. The sides of the gorge were bathed in shadows and the bloodred sunset, and a familiar stream flowed out to the spillway. She spotted Zack's motorcycle—and knew she'd come out of the mountain *exactly where she and Zack had gone in!* The second entrance—on the grade next to the stream—had been hidden by a cover of dense ferns and sagebrush.

Uta scampered down to the main path. A waxing moon and winding roadway to the dam lay to her right. She took out the phone from her backpack and punched in Spider Grandma's phone number.

"Hello," came her grandmother's excited voice.

"Grandma! It's me."

"Uta!"

"I'm down by the spillway. I'm out of the mountain. Oh, Grandma . . ." Uta burst into tears.

"What's the matter? Are you all right?"

"No . . ." she said. Terror crawled in the pit of her stomach and her hands trembled. Her grandmother was talking too fast now, half English, half Ute. Too many questions. "They got him!" Uta blurted. "The raptors got Zack! This horrible larder! Monsters! Grandma—Zack's dead!"

"Listen to me, Uta . . ."

"I left Picasso in the mountain! I left them both!"

Uta heard men's rough voices in the background. She heard her grandmother arguing with them, and she heard Dr. Boneid: "At least she's out. Where's the Norak boy?"

"UTA!" Spider Grandma shouted. "LISTEN TO ME! LISTEN CAREFULLY! I'M AT BONEID'S TRAILER AT THE TOP OF THE DAM. THEY HAVE DYNAMITE—DO YOU UNDERSTAND WHAT I'M SAYING? CAN YOU HEAR ME?"

"Grandma, what's happening?"

"Where are you exactly?"

"At the spillway. The entrance you told us to use."

"Everything's going to be all right," Spider Grandma said carefully. "Start up the road, Uta. Now. Run! They've set timers at Magic Dog Canyon!"

"What?"

"They're blowing up the shunt. It'll flood the mountain! You've got ten minutes to get out of there!"

The night fog plunged down from the dam and spilled into the gorge. Uta felt numb. She turned the phone off and put it away. She was beyond tears as she walked toward the Yamaha. Still trembling, she turned the bike around, climbed on, and hit the kick start. She knew it would be easier to drive than any of her brothers' vintage Harleys.

The motor started. She threw it into gear and headed slowly back out toward the road up to the dam. She felt as if she were in some sort of helpless trance. Stunned. In shock. She thought of Zack and began to weep. Now she thought she'd accepted his death too easily. But she had seen the blackback clutching him. Like Gonzales, he must have been eaten alive. Picasso, too. And Boneid's rush to give them and Honker—all the raptors!—a watery grave.

What would you do, Zack? she thought. What would you have done if the raptors had gotten me?

She fought to stop her tears. She knew the answer. Zack wouldn't have given up so easily—look what he'd done to find Honker! He wasn't a coward. She had seen the raptor take him, but she wasn't absolutely sure what had happened.

Ten minutes!

She stopped. After a moment, she spun the bike around, kicking up dirt, and sped back down the path *toward* the mountain. The Yamaha handled as easily as a dirt bike, and she raced up the slope to the hidden entrance. The back wheel slid from side to side, but there was enough momentum for the tires to grab onto a bed of fern and slate chips. Inside the tunnel, she opened the throttle wide, and flicked on the headlight. The motorcycle flew over the gravel and railroad ties, and raced back down toward the darkness of the gruesome larder.

Before the nasty hatchlings could catch him, Picasso had made it through a narrow opening and into a tiny alcove in the cave wall. Only one or two raptors at a time could thrust their long necks through the entrance of fallen stones. They snapped ferociously, taking turns to bite Picasso with painful cobralike strikes. Several were able to sink their needle-sharp teeth into his short white fur, but he shook them off violently, and counterattacked with swift hard nips to their snouts.

Frustrated, the hatchlings finally stopped their frenzy. They sat exhausted, staring at Picasso from the mouth of the alcove. Picasso kept his eyes on them.

Suddenly, the hatchlings started clawing frantically at the dirt and guano and entrance stones! Their forelimbs dug rapidly, like squirrels struggling to reach a cache of chestnuts. Picasso whined as the stones began to loosen and fall away.

NIGHT

*T*he eerie silence of the cave was broken by the scream of a motorcycle as Uta hurtled through the tunnel, narrowly avoiding the stalagmites, and shot into the larder chamber. The noise echoed off the walls as she crashed her way through the dripping and bloated sacks. Finally, the bike broke into the clearing in front of the towering grisly wall. She knew the raptors heard her. It was just a matter of time.

She braked to a stop, and let her eyes drift up over the cocooned prey. The bike's headlight picked up a fresh hanging form. At first she thought it was a weathered piece of wood, a bleached mass that had been sculpted like driftwood. She got off the motorcycle and walked closer. Now the beams from her helmet lit up the grisly sack like a lava lamp. It was spun of ghostly, wet, and translucent fibers wrapped tightly like bands around a mummy.

Uta reached up. She could barely touch the bottom of the hanging sack. She gasped when she recognized the distorted features. Inside, Zack's face was twisted, flattened by the filaments. She began to cry out. She wanted to brush the matted hair off his brow and close his lips from their frozen scream.

She couldn't leave his body there. She would take him down and get him out of the cave before . . .

Uta climbed onto a rise of shale and managed to grasp the bottom of the sack. She grabbed his ankles through the membrane and tried to pull the sack down, but the fibers held strong. She tried again, tugging for all she was worth, until her footing gave way and she slipped to the ground. "Forgive me, Zack," she said, stepping back. She stared up at him. For a split second she thought she saw movement. A faint twitch of a finger. She knew that there were reflexes after death, but then his chest heaved and he coughed. She thought she was hallucinating. His eyes blinked.

And *opened*!

"You're alive!" Uta cried out. "Zack! You're alive!"

She remembered the supplies in the Yamaha's saddlebags and rushed to them. She grabbed a penknife, opened it, and raced back. She sliced at the bottom of the bag. "Zack! I'll get you out!"

Uta hadn't noticed the shadow creeping up behind her. Suddenly, she felt a tightening around her waist, a pressure crushing the air out of her. Her hands dropped to grasp gnarled, thick, and clawed fingers clutching her. Savagely, she was ripped away from the sack and turned in the air.

She looked up into the roaring face of Honker's mother.

"No!" she screamed at the raptor. The claws began to cut into her. "No!"

She tried to break loose as she was lifted toward the raptor's gaping jaws. She begged, thinking she'd be understood—but she was lifted toward the jagged, terrible teeth. "I'm sorry," Uta said quickly. "I'm sorry." She made her apology, and quickly, with all of her strength, she plunged the knife into the mother's shoulder. The mother raptor roared again, this time in surprise and outrage and pain. She dropped her prey, and Uta turned to flee—but the blackback suddenly roared out of its den to block her escape. Behind her was the cave wall and a mound of sharp, fallen shale.

BAM!

A distant explosion sent a shock wave through the larder that rippled the sacks like wind crawling through a field of wheat. The blast was muted, but massive. Boneid had blown the shunt.

Picasso crouched and barked, alert as a hawk. The hatchlings had quickly undermined the narrow entrance to his alcove. Several of the snapping heads shot at him. Others were behind them, pressing forward, hissing, shrieking to be part of the kill.

A large stone was scraped away and the attackers' teeth began to find their mark. One of the hatchlings bit Picasso's neck and began to shake him like a shark trying to tear off a piece of flesh. Picasso pulled loose, but the others nipped at him again and again.

Picasso heard the sound of the motorcycle, but somewhere, better than that was another sound.

HONK.

Picasso knew an old friend was racing toward the alcove long before he saw him.

HONK. HONK. HONK.

Picasso's growl transformed into a happy bark. A new energy surged into him as he fought wildly against the horde of invading hatchlings. He was holding his own as Honker ambushed the hatchlings, rushing

144

at them from the rear. Honker was firstborn, well fed—bigger than the others.

Smarter.

He shrieked and hissed and honked until all of the smaller raptors scattered. Honker went to Picasso's side and began rubbing his head against him. Then they heard Uta's distant cries. Together, they scampered out of the alcove and raced for the heart of the larder.

Uta's screams jolted Zack into consciousness. He felt woozy from the claw thrust up through his chin. It had been like an injection.

Something deadening.

A few moments more and all of his memory returned, howling into his mind, and he realized where he was. Strength flowed back into him as he strained against the slimy, binding fibers. He tried to kick, but his legs were lashed. Below, through the weaving of the grisly sack, he saw the blackback teaming up with the mother raptor. They had Uta cornered against a wall, and he saw the terror in her face.

He heard barking.

Picasso!

Zack spotted the yapping ball of shaggy white fur running out from the labyrinth of dripping sacks. Zack called to him and saw who was at his side.

HONK. HONK.

Picasso ran under the sack and took a flying leap at the bottom of it. He swung and clawed, trying to tear a hole, but his jaws lost their grip and he fell. He jumped again, Honker along with him. Their teeth locked into the fibers, but it wasn't enough to tear the sack loose.

ROAR.

The blackback and mother raptor heard the frenzy. It disturbed them. Troubled them. They turned away from Uta and began to move toward Zack. He saw what was happening and struggled wildly—but still the bindings held! His mind raced like a computer. Desperate images. Snippets of faces and thoughts. His father. Fragments of ideas. Strategies twisted and mixed up. He thought of Uta.

And Spider Grandma and her crazy stand and the grubs and the fire and the phone and . . .

And . . .

The arrowhead in his pocket!

He wiggled and struggled, and sucked in his gut. Slowly, he managed to slide his hand down and into the pocket of his jeans. His fingers curled around the sharp edges of the stone. It began to cut into him, but he inched the arrowhead up and out, and began to slice at the sack.

The slippery bands split like packing tape against a knife blade. Covered with slime, Zack spilled out onto the floor.

The blackback and mother raptor closed on him now, lunging at him. Uta threw stones. Picasso and Honker snapped at the raptor's heels, but there was a new sound cutting across all the others. A low trembling, escalating with the force of an earthquake. The whole ground of the cave shook. Suddenly, at the far corner of the cave, a wall of water exploded up through the floor. "Bones blew a shunt!" Uta shouted to Zack.

"What?"

"A shunt! He's flooding the mountain!"

"He's crazy!" Zack yelled. He saw the Yamaha and ran to it. For a moment he thought about leaping onto it, starting it, and getting Uta—but the deluge was barreling toward him with the speed of a tidal wave. Geysers exploded from the alcoves. Fragments of limestone shot through the air like spears. The raptors, reeking of death and crusted blood, loomed above Zack as he yanked the gas hose loose from the motorcycle. He dragged the bike along on its side, the gasoline from its tank gushing out onto the ground. The raptors opened their massive jaws, but Zack grabbed one of the flares from the saddlebags, struck its lighter tip, and dropped it into the fuel.

BAM!

The raptors shrieked as a sea of bright white fire climbed up their haunches.

Zack ran to Uta. He grabbed her hand and fled with her away from the dinosaurs as the flames of the gasoline floated atop the flood. Picasso and Honker raced along behind them to a last patch of high ground. The only light now shot forward from Uta's helmet. It caught a slab of rock paintings, images of shrieking buffalo being butchered by stick figures with axes. Above one tunnel were painted demon faces with fangs and bulging evil eyes. Above another exit was the image of a dancing rope and a laughing man playing the flute.

"*This* way!" Uta yelled.

"Coming," Zack said. "Picasso! Honker!" A sharp incline kept them above the level of the rising flood-water as they raced up it. The tunnel ended at a dizzy-ing shaft with rotting railroad ties for stairs. Honker hung back now, shivering and staring at the rising torrent. He began to cry plaintively.

"What's wrong?" Zack asked.

Uta saw Honker at the water's edge. "He's looking for his mother."

"Why?"

"Who knows? She's ugly as sin, but he must have fig-ured out she's all his."

Zack groaned and picked up Honker. "Sorry, boy." He carried him up a half-dozen flights of stairs and set him back down on the ties. Picasso took over urging Honker upward. They kept ahead of the raging, rising water. They had climbed several hundred feet up the shaft when a step broke under Uta.

CRAAAAACK.

She tumbled backward toward the black hole of the shaft. Zack grabbed her arm and pulled her to him— stopping her fall into churning water. "You okay?"

"Yes," Uta said as she steadied herself and climbed back up to the broken tie. Quickly, Zack locked his hands into a cradle. She held onto his shoulders, put a foot up, and he hoisted her to a solid tie. He handed up Picasso and Honker, and scrambled up after them.

"Come on!" Uta yelled as the water rose faster. "We must be halfway up the mountain."

"We *hope*."

Honker led them now, bounding up two ties at a time. A wind howled down into their faces, and Zack knew they were near an exit. There were voices drifting down.

Men's voices.

"Listen," Zack said.

The light from Uta's helmet shot straight up the shaft.

There were pipe railings now, and ties protected with fresh linseed.

"I know where we are," Uta said. "This was part of the cave tour."

There was a loud crackle, a sound like a lightning bolt hitting a tree.

BAM! BAM! BAM!

A hail of bullets rained down splintering a wooden tie. "Rifle shots!" Uta yelled, halting the climb. "They're firing at us!" Another shot exploded the step next to Honker. "At Honker!"

"Don't shoot!" Zack called up the shaft. "Honker! Honker!"

BAM! BAM!

Sparks flew from the shaft wall and as more bullets ricocheted off into the darkness. One of the bullets whizzed by, inches from Zack's head. "Stop it!" he shouted furiously up the shaft. Whimpering and trembling, Honker ran back down toward him. Zack scooped him up and held him close to his chest.

"Boneid's gunmen won't shoot us!" Uta cried out.

"They're in the upper shafts waiting to shoot everything. They don't even know we're here! Anything that moves they think is a dino!"

"If we shield Honker, they might let him live."

Zack held the hatchling closer. "It doesn't matter. If Bones gets him, he'll turn him into some freak show and hog all the glory."

Uta directed the light from her helmet into a side tunnel she recognized. "Unless . . ."

"What?"

"We get him to the other side of the dam," she said. "To the badlands!"

"What badlands?"

"Across the dam. There's a mess of canyon lands. Cliffs and sandstone caves weave in and out like a crazy maze. There are ridges and shadowy craters, and sinkholes and crevices. It's like a crazy puzzle, rugged and craggy and forsaken. There could be a herd of elephants or wild horses living there and nobody would find them. Ever! If we set Honker loose there, that's the only place in the world where he'd be safe."

Zack thought of his father. And the dream of money. Lots of money. And fame. He thought about the dream he had of being with his friends back in L.A. again. He thought about himself and everything that had seemed so important to him. He stroked Honker's snout. The baby raptor's wide, frightened eyes looked up at him. "Couldn't they just shoot at us up there, too?"

"No! They won't expect us to come out on the east

side of the dam. Follow me," Uta said. "We don't even have to go to the top! We can go right *through* the dam!" She turned and started jogging down the tunnel she remembered from taking tourists on endless summer tours. For a few moments, Zack held back—paralyzed at the shaft. There was another crackle of rifle fire as he set Honker down, and they raced after Uta.

THE DAM

Uta and Zack reached a massive corrugated door at the end of the tunnel. "This leads to the penstock level," Uta said excitedly.

"What's in there?" Zack asked as he tried the door handle.

"It's where they let the water in to turn the turbines. The dam's got three levels. Bones is on top where the gantry crane is."

"The one on tracks?"

"Right. The crane's computer controls and opens the water gates at regular intervals. We're a couple of hundred feet below that on the pipe level. The turbines are at the bottom."

Zack grabbed the handle harder and tried lifting the door again, but it wouldn't budge. "It's motorized," Uta said, heading for a control box on the right. "You have to punch in a code. I hope they haven't changed it."

She punched in four numbers. An electric motor whirred and the door lifted in short, jerky motions. Fragments of old bird nests and dried rodents fell from its beams. Like a curtain lifting on a stage, it revealed a huge tiled room that stretched the length of the dam.

They slipped under the rising door and Zack saw the gaping mouths of a series of immense water pipes. "They're huge." Each of the five pipes had a diameter over thirty feet with a hydraulic gate above it holding back thousands—millions!—of gallons of reservoir water. Water leaked from the seals and trickled hundreds of feet down to the blades of gigantic turbines.

The door closed tight behind them as Zack and Uta walked out beneath rows of dim lightbulbs that hung from the massive vaulting ceiling.

HONK.

Zack saw the excitement in the raptor's eyes, and Uta sensed the sadness creeping into Zack.

"He smells his freedom," Uta said gently.

"I know," Zack said.

Dr. Boneid went to the main control turret of the dam to make certain the flooding was complete. He left a couple of the older Ute workers to smooth things over with the raving old Indian woman who kept shouting that there were kids in the mountain. Boneid told them, *"Give her money. Anything. Get rid of her!"* As far as he was concerned, anyone left in the bowels of Silver Mountain was dead.

At the first report of a lizard seen in the main shaft, Boneid had dispatched Manny Spencer to make certain they'd bagged it. He wanted at least one good specimen out of the hunt.

"Is it a dinosaur?" Boneid had screamed into his radio.

A trapper's voice crackled back. "All we know is that it looks like a lizard." He could tell from the trappers' voices that they weren't about to swear that they'd seen a living dinosaur. The chief engineer sat in front of the dam's main control console. "The mountain's as flooded as it's going to get, Dr. Boneid," he said.

"Good." Boneid's eye picked up a flashing white dot moving across a section of the console. "What's that?"

The engineer glanced over. "Somebody's on the penstock level."

"I didn't send anybody down there."

"They must have come in from the caves," the engineer said. "One of your men probably has the access door combination."

Boneid didn't like the idea that anybody was opening doors anywhere. He thought it might be the Kinski brothers, who had a reputation for never taking orders and screwing up everything they touched. They probably thought they'd set the bear traps wherever they felt like it.

"I'm checking it out," Dr. Boneid said, grabbing his rifle. His regular gun was a 308 Winchester, but he had borrowed a Magnum 460 for the hunt. He got into the turret elevator and pressed the button for the penstock level. The door closed, and the elevator moved slowly down the two hundred feet. When the doors opened, he saw Zack and Picasso on a platform peering into one of the penstock pipes. "Hey," he yelled. "What're you doing down here?"

Zack turned to face Boneid. Picasso growled as Boneid stepped out of the elevator holding his rifle ready.

"Point that gun away, please," Zack said, coming down the steps from the platform.

Boneid looked past Zack. Now he saw the Indian girl down by a second pipe. He knew who she was, and he remembered Zack all too well. Then he spotted Honker, and his hand began to shake. He knew that one way or another, he was going to get proof that he'd seen a living dinosaur! He aimed the rifle at Honker.

"No!" Zack yelled.

Uta moved in front of Honker. "You don't have to shoot him!" she shouted. "He won't run anywhere." Honker hissed at Boneid. Dr. Boneid glanced over to the electronic door. "How'd you two open that? How'd you get in here?"

Now there were new sounds coming from behind the door—sounds from the mine tunnel beyond. Boneid turned back to Uta and Zack. They were backing Honker farther away from him. He aimed again. "You stop where you are, or I'll shoot!" Boneid said. "None of you move! None of you!" He yanked the radio up from his belt to his lips and began shouting into it. "Manny! Bring the Kinskis ASAP! I need a cage down here at the penstock gates!"

The racket from behind the door was earsplitting, and the ground began to shake. There were shrieks and junglelike screams—a pounding that sounded like thunder. The cries of raptors reverberated in the tunnel. There was impact after impact on the door.

THUD. THUD.

Boneid was confused. The door buckled. He stepped away and dropped to one knee to hold his rifle steady. He checked a spare clip of Magnum shells as the door gave way.

CRAAAAASSH.

The door burst off its track, smashing onto the tile floor. The flame-scarred mother raptor with a pair of large adult raptors shrieked as they thundered across the crushed corrugated sheeting.

"They survived the gasoline!" Zack yelled. Uta and Picasso turned and ran with Honker for the door at the other end of the gate room. Boneid fired at the raptors as they charged straight at him. Another hatchling scurried through the ruptured doorway, skirting along the wall. Boneid fired shot after shot at the adult raptors.

BAM. BAM.

Boneid trembled with exhilaration now. He missed the charging adults, scrambled to one side, and lowered his aim trying to get the slower hatchling into his rifle sight.

"No!" Zack yelled, rushing Boneid and knocking the rifle out of his hands. "Leave them alone! This is their only way out of here! Let them go!" Boneid brought his hand back and slapped Zack to the ground. He crawled on his hands and knees to his rifle, grabbed it, and stood trying to take aim again. The raptors were past him. He spun around and fired several shots at their backs, emptying the Magnum clip. They shrieked in pain as slabs of their flesh were torn open. Blood and lymph gushed from their wounds—but still they managed to flee.

Uta reached the far end of the penstock level ahead of the panicked dinosaurs. She punched the code into the lock and the east door lifted. Boneid shoved a second clip into his rifle and fired again. He was so intent on the slaughtering he didn't notice the pounding of the massive form racing through the tunnel. Zack saw the shadow bounding through the doorway.

"Watch out!" Zack cried out.

ROAR.

The sound shook Boneid's teeth. He spun around and fired high. For a moment he saw the blistered mutant blackback with its rotting, twisted teeth—the great yellow spirals that circled up through shards of bone and dried flesh to pierce the raptor's own skull. Fluids gushed from its mouth. The blackback shot its jaws down at Boneid, closing them on his head.

"EEEEEEH. EHHHHH."

Boneid screamed as his whole body was airborne. The raptor shook his bulk right, then left. Zack heard the cracking neck bone, and one of the raptor's hind claws flew up and shredded Boneid's chest. The blackback snapped violently, throwing its head back as blood and shards of skull poured down. The raptor tossed what was left of Boneid into the gaping mouth of the pipe. Zack heard the body falling, slapping against the metal sides as it fell down to the turbines.

Zack started slowly backing toward the open door, but the blackback turned and saw him. Zack spun around and ran for his life. He heard the raptor charging after him, its feet pounding the tile and cement floor. The humongous beast was right behind him and closing fast with each of its huge leaps.

"Faster!" Uta screamed to Zack from the far doorway.

"I can't!" Zack cried, gasping as he dove right and crawled under a metal staircase. The beast stopped and started thrusting its forearms into the shadows beneath the stairs. The claws on its powerful hind limbs struck the stanchions and support pipes with brutal ferocity.

"Leave him alone!" Uta shouted as she rushed forward, trying to lure the blackback away from Zack. Picasso ran ahead of her, barking. The blackback saw them and started to charge. Zack jumped out from beneath the staircase and started screaming at the blackback. "Over here! I'm over here, you idiot!"

The blackback stopped, confused. Picasso ran right up to it, yapping wildly. The mutant raptor ignored him and slammed the staircase again, bending it. It saw Zack behind it now, and swung out at him as Picasso leaped forward and sunk his teeth into the raptor's hind leg. The giant raptor roared with outrage. It turned and with a flick of its thick tail slapped Picasso and sent him flying into a concrete wall with a sickening thud.

"No!" Zack cried out as Picasso fell into a maze of repair lights, paint cans, and tarps. The dog lay motionless, and Zack tried to get to him—but the blackback charged again. Its hind foot pounded the floor like a raging bull's, and the raptor roared with earthshaking power. The sight of the mammoth dinosaur with its slabs of muscles, colossal claws, and jagged teeth paralyzed Zack.

A siren started to wail, and a yellow light spun above the first penstock tube on the upper level. Zack broke out from the spell of terror and ran up the stairway with the blackback stalking him. Zack saw Uta was safe. She ran to Picasso and picked up his limp body. He could see she was crying as she carried Picasso toward the far gate.

"I don't know what to do!" Uta screamed to Zack.

"Save yourself!" Zack called down from the platform. As the blackback closed on him again, Zack's thoughts skipped from his father lying in a hospital bed to the dread on Uta's face and lifeless form of Picasso. The color of rage began to rush into Zack's face. His eyes became cold and hard, and he stood to face the monster. "YOU WANT ME? COME AND GET ME!" he shouted at the blackback. "COME AND GET ME!"

The raptor followed Zack onto the upper level, where the catwalks were cantilevered over the gaping mouths of the huge water pipes. He was past the first of the five penstock tubes. Its light still flashed and a chain was pulled taut. The thick metal gate started to rise. There were five seconds of clanging, a sound as if there were some imminent nuclear armageddon.

CLANG. CLANG. CLANG.

And the gate was wide open. A great torrent of water burst forth, arced into the mouth of the pipe, and plunged three hundred feet down to the screaming turbine blades.

The blackback leaped onto the metal lace of the catwalk and continued to chase its prey. Zack ran past the second penstock tube as its light automatically began to flash and the siren shrieked. Through the catwalk grating he could see the turbines below, like the blades of a giant blender. He felt the catwalk shake from the sheer tonnage of the blackback treading after him.

CLANG. CLANG. CLANG.

The gate on the second penstock gate lifted quickly.

Uta had laid Picasso's body down behind a massive tool chest. She stepped over the heavy electrical cables that led to the temporary work lights. She heard the commotion from the upper level, looked up, and her face turned pale.

Great torrents of water were cascading out of the gates into the first two giant pipes, and she saw the blackback closing on Zack.

"Run, Zack! It's right behind you!" Uta screamed.

He couldn't hear her. The third and forth penstock lights were spinning and their sirens were deafening. He felt the catwalk shaking violently and the breath of impending death on his neck. He made it to the catwalk over the fifth penstock pipe. The blackback was almost on him, and he was forced out onto a narrow walkway over the very center of the pipe. The blackback halted on the main catwalk. It seemed to know Zack was trapped, that there was nowhere else he could run.

Zack held on to the railing as the blackback made a first lunge to slash him with the claws of his forearms. The walkway shook under the creature's weight, and Zack fell down on the grating and hit his head on the railing. For a moment he was dizzy and stared down at the waiting steel blades in the pit of the abyss.

As if grinning, the blackback stepped out onto the walkway and hovered over Zack. Its spittle dripped down onto Zack's heaving chest, as it leaned down and stuck its claw into his shoulder and twisted until blood poured out. Zack screamed in agony. He felt faint as the raptor lifted him up toward its jaws. At the sight of the jagged teeth, Zack shrieked and punched at the blackback's snout. Suddenly, everything went white. Stark, burning white. For a moment, Zack was puzzled by the blackback's roaring, its tottering and flailing wildly as if it had gone blind. The raptor dropped him onto the walkway.

"Run, Zack!" he heard Uta's voice.

Zack scrambled to his feet and saw her manning a giant spotlight she'd rolled out from the work area. Its beam was slammed painfully onto the blackback's face.

CLANG. CLANG. CLANG.

The light and siren of the fifth penstock turned on, a stroboscopic madness breaking loose over its reservoir gate. The raptor swung a forelimb at him. Zack felt the walkway buckling. He knew there was only a second before high-pressure water would sweep over them and they'd be washed into the pipe. The gate started to lift, and Zack ran to the end of the walkway and leaped at the gate. It lifted higher and higher, as he grabbed onto its bands and rivets and chains—flattening himself against the gate as the wall of water arced out beneath his feet. The blackback roared and tried to retreat, but the torrent crashed down on it. The walkway shook violently now, collapsing and tumbling the monstrous raptor down, down toward the whirling blades.

"Zack! Thank God!" Uta cried as she reached a side

catwalk. She reached out, and Zack inched along the gate until he could grab her hand and jump to safety. He tried to smile, and he wrapped his arm over Uta's shoulder as they came down from the platform. They walked to the clump of white fur lying near the east door. Zack saw the happiness and relief leave Uta's eyes.

Zack dropped to his knees and petted Picasso's head. There was no movement.

"Let me," Uta said, kneeling beside him. "I've seen dogs get knocked silly by a bear. You're supposed to hold them and rub them—get the blood to flow to their heads." She took Picasso up, cradling him as she stroked his head and neck.

"Picasso," she whispered. "Picasso."

The dog slowly opened his eyes.

A wide smile crept across Zack's face. He took Picasso from Uta and followed her out of the dam and into the night. There was a break in the fog, and they could see the vast badlands that seemed to stretch on forever. They looked out past the jagged sandstone cliffs and split rock ledges that made up the maze of canyon lands. Fingers of the night fog crept down from the north cove of the reservoir.

"Honker's mother—she made it through?" Zack asked Uta.

"Yes."

"Good."

Zack set Picasso down. The dog walked a few steps and then sat down, groggily staring off into the canyons. Uta took Zack's hand and they turned back to climb up the slope toward the top of the dam.

"Come on, Picasso!" Zack said.

The dog didn't move. Uta and Zack went back to him. He turned with puzzlement in his eyes to look at Zack. Zack picked him up. They had climbed halfway up to the highway before they saw the silhouettes of Spider Grandma and Larry Ghost Coyote coming down the slope from the dam road.

"Uta! Zack!" she called to them. "Come on. It's time to go home. Come. Yes, we'll go home."

They saw that Spider Grandma held blankets and a sheepskin draped over her arms, bright moving images of painted cougars and glittering bears in the moonlight.

RETURN

*I*t was three weeks before Zack's parents were due to arrive back at the Dry Lakes airstrip aboard the twin-engine medical plane. Zack and Uta had fixed up the ranch house as best they could, but there were many deep scratches in the furniture and walls. Zack's father would easily figure out what made them.

Zack waited for Uta outside with Picasso. He could have picked her up in his parents' old Volvo station wagon that was in the garage, but she had insisted on coming for him. The staff from the dig had planned a big welcome back to greet Professor Norak at the airport. They'd thrown the event together once they'd heard the news that divers had found several of Boneid's teeth in the spillway and that the university had selected Norak as their new boss on the dig. The only other strange thing found was Gonzales's skull in an eel trap. It was said that fat black eels had shot out of the eye sockets, and that they had been feasting on the brains.

Zack and Uta were glad that outsiders had found no proof to Boneid's claims about seeing living dinosaurs. The part that puzzled Zack most was that his father couldn't remember anything about his accident. The rockslide. The doctors at Mormon Hospital had said it was normal for the mind to block things out, to repress anything that was too painful. Professor Norak remembered nothing about the cave or his mule. Nothing. They told him it was a type of post-traumatic memory loss, that it was perfectly normal, and in time he might remember everything.

And the medicines he'd received didn't help his memory either. They'd given him his own morphine drip machine and he found the painkillers worse than the pain. There had been more nightmares and a relentless depression settling into his mind, as though the medicines had literally wrapped his brain in cellophane. It had taken the last several days to get his electrolytes back in balance, but by now he was ready to face anything.

Picasso followed Zack out to the storage shed. Zack missed his Yamaha and had already started saving for a new one from his earnings at the Chile Cafe. He'd explain to his father about destroying half his spelunking equipment. He'd explain everything when his father was ready to hear it.

There was a slab of broken mirror set up on the work-table and he caught sight of himself. He wore a headband Uta had made for him the week before on a pike-fishing trip with Spider Grandma and Larry Ghost Coyote—and he really liked it. Uta had woven it with yucca strands and beads, with a row of stick-figure flute players and yellow ropes painted across the front. Zack and Uta had done a lot of things together during the last week. Swimming at Disaster Falls. Collecting malachite geodes south of Vernal.

He leaned closer to the mirror to check the scar beneath his chin. He was aware that his own memory of what had happened was fading, too. The fluids from the raptor were affecting his brain, just as they had his father. An amnesia. But Uta remembered everything, and he had her tell him the story each day so it wouldn't disappear on him completely.

There had been a few nightmares, but there were dreams and hopes, too. He had had one dream about Honker. He dreamed that he and Uta had decided to search the canyon lands. It was winter. There was a lot of snow. They had wandered into an ice cave, and Honker was there with his mother. He looked happy, bigger. He began to come toward Zack, but that was when Zack woke up.

ROAR.

Zack came out of the shed to see Uta racing toward the ranch house on one of her brother's motorcycles. It was a full-sized Harley, painted yellow with black strips and a rusted headlight in the shape of a tiger. Her hair mixed with the long, gaudy leather fringe that snapped from the handlebars. She pulled up next to Zack. They laughed and shouted hello over the racket from the bike's broken muffler.

Picasso barked—afraid he was going to be left behind—but Zack picked him up and cradled him in his shirt. He swung up behind Uta on the wide Harley seat and slipped his hands around her waist. Zack didn't think about malls or movies or pepperoni pizzas. He held on tight as Uta opened the throttle and they roared down the dirt road toward the Drive Through the Ages.